NEW BEGINNINGS IN WILLOW HEIGHTS

WILLOW HEIGHTS SERIES BOOK ONE

ABIGAIL BECK

CONTENTS

Chapter 1	1
Chapter 2	7
Chapter 3	11
Chapter 4	16
Chapter 5	22
Chapter 6	28
Chapter 7	33
Chapter 8	42
Chapter 9	49
Chapter 10	66
Chapter 11	72
Chapter 12	78
Chapter 13	87
Chapter 14	96
Chapter 15	108
Chapter 16	116
Chapter 17	122
Chapter 18	130
Chapter 19	139
Epilogue	145

CHAPTER 1

Mary Elle stood in her backyard, admiring all the hard work the team had put into making her vision come true. She had spent over a year planning this surprise birthday party for her husband, Bill. It was his big 6-0. She wanted this night to be a night they would never forget.

They had set a white party tent with a transparent vinyl roof and a dance floor up; there was a three-tier golf-themed birthday cake, a DJ and a band, a chocolate fountain, endless amounts of alcohol, fireworks, and flowers. She loved how the clear vinyl invited the night sky into the tent. It was the perfect night beneath the stars.

Mary Elle knew this would be a big year for them, and she could not wait to see all the places they would go and the things they would do. Bill had brought it up to her a few times that he planned on finally taking some time off from work.

In their 30 years of marriage, he had never taken a vacation day or called in sick. Bill had dedicated his whole life to creating a name for himself. He had built his company from the ground up. His company had always been his pride and joy. Bill had hoped that their son, Michael, would take over the firm and often mentioned it to Mary Elle in confidence, but he had never wanted to force it on him. Bill assured her he would make all their dreams come true, which included finally taking a trip to Paris.

Mary Elle could not help but smile. Her heart was overflowing with so much love. Life was good, and she was sure that it would only get better from here on out.

"I can't wait for Bill to see this!" she said to Rita, her best friend.

"He won't know what hit him," Rita replied

Mary Elle had always wanted to be a party planner, but Bill didn't think it was wise to start a business because they needed her at home. Therefore, they agreed she would continue as a stay-at-home mom. Mary Elle put her creativity to use every birthday and holiday when she went all out for her husband and kids.

"You outdid yourself this time, Mary Elle," Rita said as she looked around in amazement. Mary Elle sure knew how to throw a party. The town would talk about this party for months to come.

"We should start getting ready, Rita; the guests will arrive soon." Since they were ten years old, Rita and Mary Elle have been best friends.

Mary Elle had shown up at school one day and seen Rita being picked on by a group of older girls. Not one to back down or keep quiet, Mary Elle stepped in and defended her. They have been inseparable ever since.

"Can I help you with anything else, Mary Elle?" her assistant, Ruby, asked.

"No, Ruby. Thank you so much for helping rally all these guys together. The place looks amazing! Now get ready. We have a party to attend," Mary Elle said with a wink.

Ruby had been Mary Elle's assistant for five years. She had just graduated from college and was now on the job hunt. She was helping Mary Elle on this last soiree. Mary Elle had watched Ruby grow up alongside her daughters. When she heard that Ruby's family was having difficulty making ends meet, she tried to offer her money, but Ruby refused. She told Mary Elle she would instead work for the money.

That was when they agreed Ruby would help her with various errands twice a week. Mary Elle didn't think of Ruby as an employee, and she considered her one of her kids. She loved her dearly and would do anything to make her life easier.

Mary Elle headed upstairs to her bedroom, where Rita had already begun getting dressed. She sat at her vanity and picked up a picture frame holding a photograph of her kids. She wished they could be here now, but she understood they were all busy living their lives.

Michael, her eldest, was in California. He followed his father's example and worked in Real Estate development. Melanie was more into the arts, like Mary Elle. She was the Creative Director for a women's magazine in New York. Last, their youngest, Tiffany, was in her senior year at a university in North Carolina studying hospitality. She dreamed of someday owning a bed-and-breakfast.

Mary Elle took great pride in her kids. They were everything she had always hoped they would be. She loved how tight-knit her little family was. Her girls had always been best friends growing up, and Michael was the overprotective big brother.

Mary Elle had always yearned to have that kind of relationship with her sister, but things were the opposite. Maybe that is why Rita and Mary Elle have always been so close; they filled that void for one another.

3

Next to that picture frame was a photograph of Mary Elle and Bill on their wedding night. They had gotten married when she was only 18. Bill had been 30. She had known she would marry Bill when she laid eyes on him.

During a summer break from school, Mary Elle had been painting on her parent's front porch when she saw him pull up in his fancy sports car to the house next door. They locked eyes, and he headed over to introduce himself. He was the realtor that Mrs. Barnett, their next-door neighbor, had hired to sell her home after her husband passed away.

Bill hosted many open houses and showings for the Barnett home. Each time, Mary Elle would sit in her parent's front yard painting, and each time Bill would come over with flowers and start a conversation with her. It was not long before they went on their first date. Bill had asked Mary Elle's parents for permission to date. They had reservations at first because of their age difference, but Bill buttered them up using his charm and squashed their worries away in no time.

Three months later, on her 18th birthday, they got married, and just a few months later, they found out she was pregnant with Michael.

A light knock on the door brings Mary Elle back to reality.

"Come in!" she calls out, expecting to see Ruby walk into the room.

Instead, her daughter Melanie pokes her head into the bedroom.

"Is everyone here decent?" she asks with a sly smile.

"Mel, is that you?" Mary Elle could hardly contain her excitement as she jumped up, opened the door wide, and pulled Melanie into a deep hug.

"Oh, my god!" Mary Elle says when she notices that Tiffany and Michael are standing behind Melanie.

"My kiddies!" she pulls all three into a group hug.

"Did you know?" she asks as she turns to face Rita with happy tears in her eyes.

Rita had been standing quietly nearby, witnessing the interaction.

"Of course, but I could never spoil the surprise," Rita says as she walks over and hugs each of them.

"It's so good to be home," Tiffany says as she jumps onto her mother's king-sized bed and makes herself comfortable.

"You're telling me," Michael says as he joins her on the other side of the bed.

"Now, what are you doing getting comfortable in bed? We have a party waiting downstairs!" Mary Elle says as she tries to get everyone out of her room, but not before taking a mental picture of her kids on the bed.

It is so lovely to have them at home, just like before. Mary Elle would never admit it aloud, but she often feels lonely in her big house with her kids so far away and Bill always at work. She always sets those feelings aside by reminding herself how proud she is of each of them, their accomplishments so far, and the items still in store for them.

"Where's dad?" asked Melanie while glancing at her smartwatch.

"He's not here yet. He should be here soon. Let's get the party started while we wait. Did Everett make it?" Mary Elle asks as she guides everyone out of her room and shuts the double doors behind them.

Everett is Melanie's husband. He is a lot like Bill, very dedicated to his work, and they hardly ever see him.

"No, he had an important shoot in Alaska this week that he couldn't miss," Melanie says.

Everett is a very well-known and respected freelance photographer. He is always away working on many projects.

Melanie met him while she was styling a photoshoot he was working on for her magazine.

They eloped a month later. Bill and Mary Elle were sad to have missed their wedding, but they respected the couple's wishes. After much convincing, Melanie let Mary Elle plan a reception dinner for family and close friends.

CHAPTER 2

*A*s they make their way downstairs, they can hear the band has already started playing, the caterers are going around passing out drinks and hors d'oeuvres, and there are people on the dance floor.

Mary Elle cannot help but smile. Today is going just as planned. She looks over to the dance floor and sees Michael spinning Ruby around and her girls dancing nearby. Ruby seems to be enjoying herself, which brings a smile to Mary Elle's face.

She wishes Bill was here to see everyone. She makes her way, greeting all her guests. Everyone that she knows and loves is here. Bill is all that is missing, she thinks as she looks at her watch. He should be here by now.

She excuses herself and heads inside to call Bill. Maybe he is just running late, she thinks as she hears the line ring, but he does not answer.

"You've reached Bill. Leave a message!" Beep. She hangs up. Where are you, Bill? Bill wasn't known for being punctual for family gatherings or anything that didn't have to do with work.

Which resulted in Mary Elle spending a lot of dinners alone after Bill canceled due to work emergencies. Sometimes she went to sleep alone and woke up alone because Bill was always working late and heading to work exceptionally early. Mary Elle understood he was only trying to make a name for himself and provide for their family, so she didn't nag him about it.

But he had promised he'd be here today. She'd told him she had planned a private dinner for them, and he'd promised to be there.

"Is everything ok, Mom?" she turns to see Michael standing nearby with a concerned look.

"It's your dad, Mikey. I've been calling him, but he's not answering. Could you please try him?"

"Sure, Mom. He's probably just running late," he says as he gets his phone out of his pocket and calls his dad.

Mary Elle shifts her attention to her neighbor, Charlotte. She tries to focus on what she says, but she can't take her eyes off Michael. He is on the phone and is visibly upset.

Mary Elle excuses herself; when she is sure that she and Michael are out of earshot, she asks him if he has spoken to his dad. Michael is hesitant to answer, and she fears the worst.

Finally, Michael says, "Yes, he picked up... but he's not coming, mom."

Not coming? She must not have heard him correctly. "I'm sorry, honey; you said your dad isn't coming?"

Michael looks around, not daring to make eye contact with his mom, "Mom, let's go inside, please. There's something I need to tell you."

He leads her inside by the elbow. Mary Elle is speechless. Her mind is racing, imagining the worst. Did he have a car accident on the way to the party? She can feel her heart beating rapidly and feels dizzy.

Once Michael was sure that no one was around, he broke the news, "Mom, there is no easy way to tell you this, but dad has been having an affair, and he will spend his birthday with her."

Mary Elle felt like she'd just been hit right in the gut. At least he's not dead, but how could this be? She and Bill had just discussed what they would do once he took time off. They had planned to travel and visit all the places they'd never been to because he was always working. She had finally booked that trip to Paris they'd always wanted to go on. They were going at the end of the month. Had he only done that out of guilt?

"I'm sorry, mom." she heard Michael say, but he sounded so far away. How long had this been going on? Who was the other person? She looked over at Michael as he watched her with tears in his eyes. How could Bill not even be the one to tell her? How could he put this burden on Michael? She had so many questions darting around her head that she couldn't wait to ask Bill.

It seemed like the room was spinning. She was falling apart inside, but she knew she had to be strong for herself and her kids. Mary Elle didn't want to make Michael feel worse than she imagined he already did. Having to tell her that his father was having an affair was hard enough. She gathered all her strength and blinked away the tears threatening to escape her blue eyes. She couldn't break down now, not in front of Michael.

"It's ok, sweetie, let's go have a good time." She said and walked out of the house before Michael could protest.

The music was blasting; the band was making everyone dance, and she knew she had to force a smile on her face. Mary Elle hoped no one noticed her absence while Michael gave her the bad news. She wanted everyone present to enjoy the night she had so lovingly prepared for Bill. Bill had never been big on birthdays or celebrations, but he always loved the themes she came up with.

Mary Elle shook the memories out of her head and walked back to celebrate another year for Bill with all of their friends. She felt nervous. She didn't want to be asked about Bill. What would she answer when they asked? There was no time. She had to muster up all her strength and fake a smile and let the guests know Bill was a no-show.

CHAPTER 3

Tiffany watched as her mother stood on the stage next to the DJ with a microphone in hand, preparing to make an announcement. Mary Elle didn't look like her usual confident self, Tiffany noted.

Her mom usually thrived in these situations. There was nothing that her mom enjoyed more than having elaborate parties for their family. As she observed her mother, she noticed she was fidgeting with the microphone. Tiffany looked around but didn't see her father anywhere. Why would her mom start a birthday speech if dad wasn't there yet?

"I would like to thank you all for coming tonight," Mary Elle began as she looked around at all the familiar faces with a weary smile, "This night might not be going exactly as planned, but it will be a night that we will always remember." She took a deep breath before continuing, "Bill will not be joining us tonight due to work. But I am sure that wherever he is - he can feel all your love and well wishes. Have a great time, everyone!"

The crowd, though confused, clapped and followed Mary

Elle's orders to have a great time. Others might not have noticed, but her mom's voice had been shaky, and something seemed off about her. This can't be right; Tiffany thought as she watched her mom hand the microphone back to the DJ and quickly made her way off the stage. Tiffany looked over to Melanie, standing next to her, and she had an equally confused look on her face. Without a word, they took off after their mother.

"Mom! Wait up." Tiffany said as they tried to catch up to her, but Mary Elle kept going.

It wasn't until they were in the kitchen that they finally caught up. "Mom, what's wrong? Where's dad?" Melanie asked.

Mary Elle had her back to them as she gripped the counter's edge for support, but Tiffany could see her shoulders shaking.

Melanie again asked, "What's wrong, mom?"

Was mom crying? Did something happen to dad? Tiffany's stomach dropped as she felt tears gathering in her eyes. She tried to calm herself and reassure herself that everything was okay.

She told herself that maybe mom was only upset that dad wasn't coming to the party. Dad had always been a workaholic and often missed out on many family functions. Perhaps he'd forgotten it was his birthday and worked late. Everyone knew that work was always their dad's top priority.

Still, Tiffany couldn't shake the awful feeling in the pit of her stomach. Michael and Melanie had always picked on her from a young age, saying she was paranoid because she was constantly worrying about this and that. She couldn't help it; everyone knew she was a worrywart. She was always overly cautious and always ready for any emergency.

NEW BEGINNINGS IN WILLOW HEIGHTS

"Are you okay?" Melanie asked as she walked past Tiffany and rested a hand on her mother's shoulder.

"I'm not sure," Mary Elle said, her voice barely a whisper.

The caterers came into the kitchen, and Tiffany pulled on her mom's arm and led her away from the kitchen to the family room. "Come, let's go sit down, Mom."

Their mom took a seat on the sectional sofa in their family room, and Melanie sat next to her. Tiffany didn't think she could sit still and stood across the room.

"What's wrong, mom? Did something happen to dad?" Melanie asked again.

Tiffany stood back and observed her mother. She had never seen her cry. She didn't know what to think, but they wouldn't still be here if something had happened to dad. They would be on their way to wherever he was.

"Mom, you're worrying me. Did something happen to Dad?"

"No, your dad is okay." her mom said with a sad smile without meeting her eyes.

"What is it? Please tell us."

* * *

MARY ELLE intensely disliked appearing weak, especially in front of her kids. She hoped she was getting ahead of the drama by making the announcement. Her daughters, of course, had seen right through her.

She needed to get it together. She was still processing what she had just found out. How could she tell them their family was being ripped apart? Many things came into Mary Elle's mind about missed events, and she couldn't help but wonder if it hadn't been "work" keeping Bill away. How long had he fooled her? Who else knew of this affair?

She didn't know how to break the news to them. Mary

Elle didn't want to ruin their night either, but she didn't like the girls worrying about Bill. She was trying to find the right words to tell them that Bill wasn't there because he would rather spend his birthday with his new lover, whoever she was. Mary Elle didn't want to open the floodgates of emotions and tears, not while the party and guests were still there. She didn't want to appear a victim either.

She took pride in showing her girls to be independent and strong, but this was killing her. The heartbreak she felt was almost unbearable. She loved Bill so much. They had grown up together and had worked hard to build this life and family. Now, it's all gone. How could he throw it all away? She wiped the tears away as she looked at her daughters' concerned faces.

Finally, she said, "Girls, there is a lot that we need to discuss, but we should wait until later. People are going to wonder where we are."

"No. You are upset, and we deserve to know what is going on." Melanie said.

Melanie had always been the most hotheaded one out of all her kids. Especially for their family. Mary Elle had been just as aggressive at her age but had learned to cool off as the years had gone by.

Mary Elle sighed in resignation; she knew Melanie wouldn't let this go. So she tried to think of the best way to break the news.

She stood up and made her way to the mantle above the fireplace adorned with photos of their family throughout the years. Michael had made the mantle when he got into wood-working, thanks to his high school instructor.

Her heart ached as she looked at the photos. Like any family, they had been through hard times, but she always knew they could get through anything together, but how would they get through this now?

Mary Elle turned to face her daughters and said, "Your dad is not coming tonight, but don't worry, he is fine," she held her hand up to calm them down. "He will spend his birthday with someone else."

"With someone else? Who?" Melanie asked.

"I don't know yet. I haven't talked to him," Mary Elle hated how ridiculous that sounded. Her marriage was over, and she didn't even know how or why or even who her husband was leaving her for.

"So, how do you know this?" Tiffany asked gently as she made her way over to her mother and took her hand in hers.

Mary Elle looked down at their hands before continuing, "He asked Michael to let me know. Now let's go out there. We have a party waiting." Mary Elle said as she tried to muster up a smile.

"I can't believe him!" Melanie said and stormed off in search of Michael.

CHAPTER 4

"Are you sure you want to go back out there? I can tell them you caught a stomach bug or something." Tiffany said as she eyed her mother.

"It's fine, honey. No one needs to know what is going on tonight. We can still salvage this night and try to make the best of it."

Tiffany knew she should try harder to sway her mom, but it wouldn't be possible without her sibling's help. Their mother was stubborn, and once she had her mind made up, it was hard to get her to do anything else.

Instead, she followed closely behind her and promised herself that she'd be there for her every step of the way, the same way their mother had always been there for them.

Tiffany stayed by her mom's side for the rest of the night. She stepped in whenever anyone asked about her dad. If her mom didn't want anyone to know tonight, she made sure no one found out. No one found it strange that Tiffany had taken over answering questions about her dad like a hawk, and if they did, they said nothing.

Tiffany was honestly still in shock over everything that

had happened that night. Bill had never been a cheater or an inadequate father - at least not that they knew of. He wasn't the most attentive dad, but he had always provided for them. She knew that her dad worked hard so that their family could live comfortably.

Tiffany couldn't wrap her head around his decision. Why would he do this now? Was he going through a midlife crisis? Who was this other woman? Why did he decide tonight would be the night to call it quits?

She made the mistake of mentioning this in passing to Melanie during the party, to which Melanie responded, "There is no excuse for what he's done to mom. I will never forgive him!" Tiffany hoped no one had heard her. That was the difference between Melanie and Tiffany - Tiffany always tried to put herself in other people's shoes and see what had led them to take the actions they'd chosen; At the same time, Melanie only reacted to the outcome, and if the product were something that negatively affected their family, well, her reaction wouldn't be pretty. She didn't like what her father had done or what it would do to her family, but she knew she'd still want her father in her life, regardless.

ONCE EVERYONE WAS, Mary Elle and her kids gathered in the living room.

"How long have you known?" Melanie asks Michael again, eyeing him suspiciously.

Not fazed by her accusatory tone, Michael looked around, trying to find the right words. He couldn't believe his dad had put him in this place, but he felt a great responsibility to keep everything under control. He couldn't sit by and watch his family fall apart.

"As you all know, Dad flew to San Francisco last week to

see me. I could tell something was heavy on his mind, and after much prodding, he told me he'd been seeing someone, but he promised he would come clean as soon as he returned home." He looked over at his mom. "I'm sorry, mom. I tried to convince him to tell you. I called him every day and reminded him he'd promised me he'd tell you."

Mary Elle nodded and said, "I remember, I thought it was odd that Bill would fly to California without me, but he had said he only wanted Michael's input on a project he was working on. Since it was only a day trip, he didn't think I would want to go." she went over to Michael and sat next to him, covering his hands with hers. "It's okay, honey. It's not your fault at all."

"Did he say who the other woman is?" Tiffany asked softly.

"Yes, who is this home-wrecker?" Melanie demanded to know.

Michael braced himself for their reactions. He knew this would not be good. "Yes, it's Barbara Krieger," he said as he shook his head.

"Well, I can't say I'm surprised." Melanie said, "Since we were little, whenever Dad would drop us off at school, she'd always rush over and try to get his attention. You remember, right, Michael?"

He nodded but didn't say a word.

"It's been an eventful day, kids. Let's get some rest," Mary Elle said as she stood and made her way upstairs, leaving Michael and his sisters behind.

* * *

ONCE UPSTAIRS, Mary Elle grabbed a set of clean pajamas and headed to the shower. In the shower, she let herself fall apart. It hadn't been easy holding it together all night, but she did what she had to do for her family. Mary Elle searched for a sign in her mind that would clue her in on what had happened. She had noticed he had become distant but had brushed that idea off a while back.

How long had this been going on? Had Bill always been unhappy with their life together? How could she have been so clueless? Life had slowed down drastically once the kids moved away, but she always thought they were happy.

Once she'd heard Michael utter her name, everything had gone black. Mary Elle listened to her kids talking in the background, but she was lost in thought. Barbara Krieger. It was bad enough that Bill was unfaithful, but with Barb? Of all people?

Mary Elle and Barbara had grown up together, and they'd always had a friendly competition going on with each other. At least Mary Elle thought it had been friendly. Maybe this whole time, she'd been wrong.

If Mary Elle had a party, then Barbara had one the week after, and it was always bigger and more extravagant than Mary Elle's. Barbara was a widow; she had a son named Timothy. Michael and Tim were the same age. They went to the same school and played on the football team in high school, but they weren't close friends.

Barbara's husband died when Timothy was very young in a tragic car accident. There had been many rumors about Barbara and men after her husband died, but none of them ever stuck around.

Barbara was always jealous of Mary Elle. People in town knew there was drama between them, but no one quite understood why. Barbara and Mary Elle had been friends until Rita moved into town. Barbara and another group of girls bullied Rita, and Mary Elle stepped in. This changed the dynamic of their friendship and left Barbara ridiculed and embarrassed. This is where it all began.

Barbara liked Mary Elle's neighbor Jacob when they were teenagers, so Mary Elle told him that Barbara still wet the bed. Very childish, but when you are young and dumb, something like that seems monumental. It also didn't help that Mary Elle's brief comment killed Barb's image with Jacob, who would smile awkwardly whenever he saw her.

Over the years, Mary Elle heard comments here and there about rumors Barbara had started about her, but she never considered it as anything other than gossip. The people in this town loved to talk, and Mary Elle was not the type of person to pay it any mind. She only focused her energy on her family. Her kids and her husband were the only things worth worrying about in her mind.

A sob escaped her as she pressed her back against the shower wall and slid down to the shower floor. Bill had been her entire world for so long. How would she go on without him? What did this mean for their family? How would this affect the kids and their relationships?

The tears just rolled down her face. She had to let it out; she couldn't hold it in. This was her alone time and where she could let the water take her tears and sadness away. She had never felt this kind of heartbreak before. Bill was her only boyfriend and her only love. She never in a million years thought he would betray her, not like this, not with Barbara. It felt as if someone was squeezing her heart. She felt the pain so deep inside her.

She knew that this could break her if she allowed it to consume her. She knew life wouldn't be the same, but she had to go on. This might be the end of one chapter, but not the story. Thoughts about the future crept in. She had never considered moving forward without Bill. He was her rock, her everything. But now, she had to depend on herself.

She gave herself a few more minutes in the shower until it was time to put her brave face back on. She took her time drying herself and lathering on with her favorite lavender lotion. Bill hated the scent, so she was always careful not to overdo it, but now she could put on as much as she wanted. She was trying to look on the bright side, reminding herself of the things she wouldn't allow herself not to bother him.

Mary Elle made her way to her nightstand and saw that she had 20 missed calls and a lot more unread text messages. She put her phone on silent and flipped the phone around so she wouldn't see any incoming calls or messages. She didn't want to read them.

Instead, she thought of the Paris trip. She had imagined it to be the most romantic trip she and Bill would ever have. After all, Paris is the city of love. Now, she thought of it as a necessary trip where she could explore love, self-love, and all the great things life had to offer. She had given Bill so much love. He was her first everything. She thought he was the love of her life, her soulmate. But how could a soulmate cheat on you and desert you?

She started thinking of who could replace Bill on this trip. Mary Elle knew her kids wouldn't want to go with her since they had jobs and things going on in their lives. She thought of Rita and would ask her if she could join her on her trip to Paris, although it was short notice. This gave her something to look forward to and lifted her spirits. Mary Elle had learned long ago not to dwell on the negative but always to find the positive in each situation. Everything happens for a reason.

CHAPTER 5

"So, is this why you insisted we all come to this party?" Melanie asked Michael as they sat in her old bedroom. Her parents had kept the room precisely the same. They had kept the walls adorned with posters of her favorite movies, and the shelves still held her many awards from school.

"Yes, I didn't know this was going to happen. I was hoping he would tell her before the party. The last time I spoke to him, he said he'd tell her after the party, but I guess he reconsidered."

"I can't believe him," Melanie said as she paced back and forth. "You know, I knew he would win no awards for father or husband of the year, but this is a new low!"

"Keep it down!" Tiffany instructed; Melanie knew Tiffany didn't want their mom to be more upset than she already was. But she couldn't keep it down.

Melanie had a fire burning inside her. She'd never felt so upset in her life. She never in a million years would've imagined that their dad would do this.

"How could he do this? How could he not even have the

decency to tell mom himself?" Melanie couldn't sit still. She was pacing back and forth and only stopped because she heard Tiffany let out a small gasp. She stopped and looked at her siblings, who were currently staring at their phones. "What is it?"

Tiffany didn't say a word and only turned her phone to show Melanie what they had seen.

Barbara had posted photos of herself and their father on his boat, celebrating his birthday.

Happy birthday, my love. I am so blessed to celebrate this year with you. I cannot wait to celebrate many more by your side.

Melanie's blood was boiling. How dare she? She grabbed the first thing she could and threw it across the room. If her parents, the pure image of a perfect marriage, couldn't make it, how could anyone else?

She'd grown up listening to her parents' love story and dreamt of sharing her own with her kids one day. She thought she'd found that with Everett. The main reason she fell for him was that he reminded her so much of her father.

He was hard working and focused. He never lost sight of his goals, which had pushed her to exceed in her career. With her parents' marriage falling apart... everything she'd ever dreamed of seemed like a lie.

"We should go check on Mom," Tiffany said, breaking into Melanie's thoughts. She watched as she gathered her things and headed to their mother's room, and she followed close behind Michael.

Melanie couldn't believe her father had cheated on her mother, but what bothered her the most was the coward he'd been by making Michael tell Mary Elle about the affair. It's so unbelievably selfish, she thought to herself.

Melanie knew marriages weren't easy. She had her problems and difficulties in her marriage with Everett, but they had agreed to talk things out and be honest with each other.

ABIGAIL BECK

She loved her parent's love story. It was like a fairytale for her. Melanie adored her father and how he had swept Mary Elle off her feet when they first met. She wondered when things had changed.

When they were little kids, she remembered that their mother would take them to the beach, and Bill always promised to be there, but work always got in the way. Still, she didn't remember him being so distant before; he wasn't a cheater or a coward, so what happened? What changed?

* * *

MARY ELLE WAS in bed writing in her journal when her kids stormed into her room. This is where she lets out a lot of her frustrations and worries.

"Mom, have you been online tonight?" Melanie asked as soon as she stepped into the room.

"No, I haven't, but I saw I had lots of missed calls and text messages. I can't look through them right now." Mary Elle answered.

All three kids looked at each other, which piqued Mary Elle's interest.

"What's going on?" She asked them.

Michael quickly got closer to his mother, followed by Tiffany and Melanie.

He leaned in and showed her the social media post Barbara had made.

Mary Elle didn't flinch. She expected Barbara to do something like this to show Bill off. Of course, she would want everyone to know she had won.

"I'm not surprised," Mary Elle finally said.

"It's so predictable. Barbara's always competing with me. She knew I would have planned something big for Bill's 60th birthday. She knew this, which is the stupid game she's

24

started since we were younger. I can't believe Bill went along with it this time."

Mary Elle turned to her phone and realized people were texting her about the post Barbara uploaded during the party. She felt like a fool.

Barbara had finally won. She outdid Mary Elle in the cruelest way possible. As she checked her text messages, Mary Elle saw Rita's messages and knew she was desperately trying to contact her.

"Are you ok, mom?" Tiffany asked quietly.

Mary Elle was trying so hard to hold back her tears. "Yes, I'm fine. I have to keep my head up," she said, and she knew she had to do just that.

They all hugged Mary Elle and gave her words of encouragement and love. She hadn't felt this kind of tenderness since they were tiny. They would always sense when she needed a "pick-me-up hug," wrapping their little arms around her neck. She missed those days when they were so tiny and caring, and they lived at home.

Mary Elle was distraught. She was livid, but she couldn't let her kids see that. Bill was their father and always would be, regardless of his life decisions. She needed to focus on something else.

"Thank you, guys; you truly are the best parts of your father and me," she said. She loved them all so much. She was crying tears of joy from the love she received in that embrace.

"So, I was thinking, my Paris trip is coming up, and I don't want the tickets to go to waste," she said as she sat up. She needed to talk about something else before she broke down in front of her kids. "I know you three have a lot going on with work, school, marriage, and various projects, so I was thinking of asking Rita to go on the trip with me. I know it's out of nowhere, but I'm hoping she'll come with me."

"That's great, mom. This is exactly what you need. It's time for you to put yourself first for once. You've always put dad and us ahead of your wants and needs. It's time for you to stop holding yourself back and focus on yourself," Tiffany said as she hugged her mother.

Melanie and Tiffany continued to encourage Mary Elle to go on the trip. They believed Rita would be the perfect person to go with her. Michael thought she should stay in town and relax here. He was worried she would miss any chance of reconciliation with Bill, but it was clear he wasn't thinking or planning on coming back to Mary Elle.

Tiffany and Melanie expressed their relief to see that Mary Elle wanted to move forward and not dwell in her pain and current situation. They volunteered to make all the arrangements to take Mary Elle to the airport and pick her up when she arrived.

THE REST of the week dragged on for Mary Elle. She loved having her kids around, but she wished it were under different circumstances. All she wanted to do was sit around and be sad while eating her favorite pistachio chocolates. It was exhausting for her to fight back the tears constantly and try to appear strong. When the end of the week approached, her kids prepared to return to their everyday lives. Mary Elle would miss them, but she needed to be alone. She wanted time to adjust to her new life and, finally, take some time to process everything.

"I can stay with you, Mom," Tiffany said as she stood in the doorway, not wanting to leave her mom alone.

"No, darling, it's ok. Don't worry about me - I'll be fine. This is your last semester, honey. Go on and make us proud."

"Are you sure? I don't think you should be alone right now."

Was she sure? She wasn't sure of anything anymore, but she knew her kids needed to go on with their lives. They had dreams and aspirations that went far beyond putting their lives on pause to watch over her. She had done that with Bill. She had put all her hopes and dreams on hold to make his dreams come true. Mary Elle refused to do that to her kids.

"It's fine. Rita will stay with me. I love you, Tiff. Don't worry about me."

The taxi driver honked at Tiffany. Melanie and Michael were already in the taxi's backseat waiting for her. She hugged her mother and reluctantly joined her siblings.

"We love you, mom!" Melanie called out as they drove off.

"Love you more!" Mary Elle called out after them.

As soon as they drove off, Mary Elle was on the go. There was only one thing on her mind, and she was a woman with a mission. She knew she could never come to terms with what happened if she did not speak to Bill first. She was going to find Bill and talk with him once and for all.

The kids had told her she should wait for their dad to reach out to her. A week later, and still no sign of him, she couldn't wait any longer. She got dressed and headed to his office.

Mary Elle looked her very best. She wouldn't allow him to see her in pain. She didn't want Barbara to know she was heartbroken, either. Mary Elle did her hair and makeup and even took time to do her nails. She looked good, and she felt good. She thought she would give him one last look at what he left behind. There's no looking back or going back. Not when he was with Barbara. Mary Elle wore her best clothes and wore her favorite perfume. She was also wearing red lipstick; Bill always liked it when she wore her red lips.

CHAPTER 6

Once she arrived at Bill's office, Angeline, the receptionist, spotted her right away. She said nothing, but Mary Elle noticed the slight swift in her demeanor. Mary Elle never missed a beat; she loved people watching and always saw the slightest change in a person. It was hard for her to understand what had gone wrong with Bill.

"Mary Elle, it's so nice to see you!" Angeline said as she stood to greet her.

"Hi Angie, you're looking great, as always. Is Bill around?"

"He's in his office. Let me page him for you." Angeline said as she reached for the phone.

"No need. I'll head right in." Mary Elle said as she walked past Angeline before she could protest. She walked into Bill's office without knocking.

She was unsure what she was expecting, but it wasn't what she saw. Bill was standing over his desk, reviewing plans for a new shopping center he was working on. He didn't look up right away, which gave Mary Elle time to study him.

He looked disheveled, not his usual put-together self. He

hadn't shaved, and his shirt was untucked. Bill had always taken great pride in how he presented himself.

His suits were always in pristine condition, and he never had a single hair out of place. He always believed that his appearance represented his business and how he ran it, and he wanted no one to think that his company was anything but the best.

Mary Elle studied him. He had always been a handsome man, and age hadn't made him any less attractive. Everything about him was familiar to her. He was the only man she had ever loved.

His eyes widened when he looked up and realized that Mary Elle was standing before him.

"Ellie." He said as he motioned for her to take a seat.

It hurt to hear him call her that. Growing up, that was the nickname her father had given her. When Bill began calling her that, it only seemed natural. Now it felt like a jab to the heart.

"I'd rather stand." She said, not taking her eyes off him.

"Mary Elle... I am so sorry about what happened. I've wanted to reach out to you, but I don't even know what to say."

At that moment, tears started coming out of his eyes, and he took a seat at his desk. Mary Elle could see that he was having a hard time, and this situation was also affecting him. She hadn't expected him to react this way.

She thought she hadn't heard from him because he was too busy being swept away by Barbara. Too busy being madly in love with her frenemy to pick up the phone and call her. She wanted to reach out to console him, to tell him it was okay, but it was not okay, and she could not forgive him.

"Why don't you tell me how you let this happen?" Mary Elle said, trying her best to stand firm. She would not let him off the hook without knowing how he could tear their family apart.

Bill sat there without saying a word, trying to gather his thoughts.

Finally, he said, "Well, remember that hotel downtown my firm worked on? Barbara was the interior designer for the project. We bonded over meetings we had to discuss the project. At first, I thought nothing of it... I could be friends with a female without it meaning anything, right?" He said as he cleared his throat and grabbed a glass of water for himself and Mary Elle from the credenza next to his desk.

"As time went on, I noticed maybe I enjoyed her company a little too much. I tried to keep my distance from her, but then we worked on a few more projects together... well, my feelings got too hard to ignore."

Mary Elle could not believe what she was hearing. She'd thought this had only happened recently, but the downtown project had been over a year ago! How did she not catch this? How could he have been lying to her all along?

"Ellie..." She flinched as he said her nickname and took a step back. He cleared his throat, "Mary Elle... I've never stopped loving you, but I am not in love with you. I never wanted to hurt you. You and the kids... you're my universe."

"How could you do this to us, then?"

He sighed and ran his hands through his hair. "I never thought that I could leave you, never thought that I could find love again. I never thought I could let myself love another woman. As time edged closer to my 60th birthday, I knew I couldn't hold my feelings back. I wanted to live. I wanted to feel excited, and Barbara makes me feel that way." As he stopped pacing and stood in front of Mary Elle, he said, "If you're honest with yourself, you'll realize that you're not in love with me anymore. You might love me. You might love the life we have together and our family, but you're not in love with me."

He was right. Mary Elle wasn't in love with him anymore, but she had made a vow–till death do us part, and she'd meant it.

She might not have been in love with him anymore, but she still loved him and their life together. Bill was her best friend, the person she knew would always be there for her no matter what, except he wouldn't be anymore. He would be Barbara's best friend now; he would be there for Barbara now, and Mary Elle would only be a distant memory of a past life for him, which broke her heart.

"Mary Elle, what I did was wrong, and believe me, I wish I could redo this. I wish I could've been honest with you from the start. However, it is too late for that now. We can only move forward, and I sincerely hope to earn your forgiveness someday." He turned and pulled out a folder from a file cabinet. "Take this," He said, handing her the file folder. "I've run the numbers, and you will get a decent amount with the divorce. You will not have a thing to worry about. You can stay in the house until you find a new place. Once you are ready, we can sell it and split the profits. Have your lawyer review everything for you."

She didn't know what to say. He caught her completely off guard. Bill had already worked everything out. He was ready to move on. How could her whole life be falling apart in just a matter of days?

* * *

MARY ELLE WALKED out of Bill's office feeling more conflicted than before. She understood where Bill was coming from, and she saw that this hadn't been easy on him either. However, it still hurt, and there certainly must have been a better way to handle all of this. She knew that for the good of their family, they would at least need to be amicable to one another... but she was not ready to forgive him just yet.

Mary Elle stopped at a flower shop and picked up a bouquet of hydrangeas, her favorite. She recalled how she and Bill had planted hydrangeas in the front yard thirty years ago at their starter home. They'd been a pain to grow, but they'd been able to make them flourish together. Too bad they had not had the same fate with their marriage. Alone, in her car, in the parking lot of the flower shop, she broke down and cried again.

As soon as she got home, she put the hydrangeas in a vase and placed them as a centerpiece on her marble kitchen island. Mary Elle set a quiche she had prepared earlier in the oven while waiting for Rita to come over.

She hadn't been able to speak to Rita since this all happened. She'd only responded quickly to a text message from her asking if it was true about Bill and Barbara, to which Mary Elle had replied, "Yes." Before leaving, Melanie had called Rita and arranged for her to stay with her for the next few days. Mary Elle couldn't wait to surprise Rita with the Paris trip; at least she had that to look forward to.

CHAPTER 7

Rita didn't know what had possessed Bill to leave Mary Elle for Barbara. Rita might be biased, but Barbara was no match to the woman that Mary Elle was in her eyes.

Barb wasn't like Mary Elle. She loved to gossip, and many times, she was the one that started all the rumors and drama that went around their small town of Helena Springs.

Rita felt guilty that she'd never brought up what Beth had told her to Mary Elle. She had never imagined that Bill would do something like this. Rita had been around when Mary Elle met Bill. She knew how crazy they were about each other. Everyone in their small town could see how in love they were. They surprised no one when they got married three short months later. "You can't fight what is meant to be," Rita's mother had said about Bill and Mary Elle. How could they all have been so wrong?

Rita arrived at Mary Elle's right on time. She parked in the circular driveway and took a deep breath, trying to calm her nerves while gripping the steering wheel. She had to come clean to Mary Elle, but she didn't know how her long-time friend would take this information. Would it upset her? Would this ruin their lifelong friendship?

Mary Elle must have been waiting by the door because she opened it right up and made her way to Rita's car.

"Here goes nothing, "Rita said as she climbed out of her SUV.

"Rita!" Mary Elle exclaimed as she pulled her into a hug.

"How are you feeling?" Rita asked her as she pulled her weekender bag out of her car. It surprised her to see that Mary Elle was in good spirits, not what she was expecting. She was dressed up and was even wearing red lipstick.

"As expected, but there is so much we need to talk about." Mary Elle said as they made their way inside. Rita felt her stomach drop. Did Mary Elle know what Beth had told her?

Once inside, Mary Elle headed into the kitchen, and Rita followed close behind.

"I prepared your favorite quiche," Mary Elle said as she pulled it out of the oven.

Rita felt her stomach do another flip. She wasn't hungry. Her nerves were acting up. She knew she had to come clean to Mary Elle. She decided it was best to rip the Band-Aid off and deal with the consequences.

"Mary Elle, there's something we need to talk about."

Mary Elle's face dropped. "Is everything okay? You don't look so well. What's wrong?"

Rita cleared her throat. She had to get this out before she broke down. The guilt was killing her. "Ellie, I feel terrible about what happened with Bill,"

"Rita, there's nothing you could've done."

"But... there is!"

"What do you mean?"

"Beth told me she'd seen Bill and Barbara looking cozy over dinner one night. I thought nothing of it. I never thought Bill could do this. Now I feel like such a fool. I could've saved you from this heartache,"

"Oh, Rita," Mary Elle said as she pulled her friend into a hug, "Please don't beat yourself up over this. Bill was the one that cheated, not you or anyone else. He knew better."

"You're not mad at me?" Rita asked as she studied Mary Elle's face.

"Of course not!" Mary Elle said as she walked away and pulled a small, long box out of a drawer. "This is for you," she said, handing the box to Rita.

"What is it?"

"Open it," Mary Elle said.

Rita carefully opened the box and let out a small gasp when she saw what was inside.

"A plane ticket to Paris?" she asked, searching Mary Elle's face for answers.

"We're going to Paris in 3 days!" Mary Elle exclaimed.

Rita couldn't believe it. She'd never been to Paris. Apart from a couple of summers away in nearby towns, she'd never stepped out of Helena Springs.

She and Bob led a modest life. Jetting off to Paris had never even seemed like a possibility. Mary Elle told Rita she and Bill had planned to fly to Paris at the end of the month. Thanks to travel insurance, she could cancel those flights and book new ones for herself and Rita.

Rita and Mary Elle spent the night planning their trip. They read reviews for all the restaurants they wanted to visit. They found travel blogs and watched travel videos that helped them plan an itinerary. Rita felt like they were young again. They spent the night scrapbooking and working on vision boards while sprawled on their bedroom floors, just as they had when they were kids. She couldn't wait to visit the city of lights. Rita even added a countdown on her phone.

ABIGAIL BECK

* * *

THE DAY HAS FINALLY COME for the ladies to jet off to the city of lights. Rita started her morning by driving over to Mary Elle's house to depart to the airport together. She brought a small box of warm chocolate croissants with her.

"Good morning, sunshine! I'm so excited we are finally going to Paris!" Mary Elle says as she greets her at the door.

She's wearing a black beret, a striped shirt, and black cropped pants. Rita can't help but smile. It is just like Mary Elle dressing up.

"I'm beyond ready to start this much-needed vacation!" Rita replies.

"The taxi should be here in no time," Mary Elle says as she pours a coffee for Rita, and they sit down to enjoy the croissants. The taxi shows up shortly after, and once they've gotten their luggage in and are en route to the airport, Rita says, "I called Bob to remind him we're leaving for Paris today and that he has to pick us up when we return. He's on a business trip but will be back when we arrive home."

THE AIRPORT CHECK-IN was a breeze and the waiting time to board wasn't bad at all. The food on the plane was pretty good for such a long trip.

Getting the luggage and taking the train through Paris was a great way to see the city and feel what to expect.

"They have a great train and subway system here. Reminds me of NYC," Mary Elle said

"It's as dreamy as it is in the movies," Rita said as she took in all the beautiful architecture.

She felt like a kid. She was giddy and didn't know which way to look because everything was beautiful. Rita is so excited to be here, and never in a million years would've imagined this would be her life.

She looks over at Mary Elle and wonders what she's thinking. She hopes she will enjoy this trip even though she was initially meant to be here with Bill.

The ladies soon arrive at the chateau and check-in. The hotel is exquisite and has a magnificent view of the Eiffel Tower. Jet lag isn't as bad as expected, but they take a quick nap to recharge.

Once they wake up from their nap, they decide to go out to dinner in a nearby restaurant and enjoy French cuisine and wine.

"Can you believe we're here?" Mary Elle asks as she looks around the small Paris Street.

"It feels like a dream, and I don't want to wake up," Rita says.

They had settled on a small restaurant next to their hotel. They had played it safe with their entrees, but they had agreed to try the escargot on the menu since they were in France. Being from a small town outside of Atlanta, Rita wasn't used to trying different cuisines. Once the server placed the small plate in the center of their table, both Mary Elle and Rita sat up.

"Are you ready?" Mary Elle asks with a devious smile

Rita downs her wine glass and slams it down on the small table. "Ready!" she says.

Both ladies grab a piece and savor it.

"That was surprisingly good." Marry Elle called the server over to their table to order another.

"Not sure what I was expecting, but I can say it's not bad."

. . .

ABIGAIL BECK

THE FOLLOWING DAY, both ladies are up bright and early. They are too excited to sleep in. The plan for the day is to visit The Louvre Museum.

While waiting in line to buy tickets for the museum, they practice how to ask to purchase tickets using a French translator app on their phone. Each time they repeat what the phone says, they break out in giggles.

"We are terrible at this!" Rita exclaims

"Didn't you take French in high school?"

"I only passed because I copied off of Charlotte!"

"That explains a lot." Mary Elle says with a sly smile

When they finally reach the teller, Rita embarrassingly stutters, asking for two tickets in French.

The teller rolls her eyes and tells her the amount due in English.

"Wow, the artwork in the museum is phenomenal," Rita says as they wander around the museum.

"All the art pieces of old are here. We finally found the Mona Lisa!" Mary Elle says with glee.

"I always thought she would be bigger. Maybe they have the section roped off, and we are about 100 ft away from the actual painting."

"I wonder why it's roped off. Might be for security."

"Such a vast museum to explore, Mary Elle, and I'm so lucky to be here!" Rita said as she hugged her best friend.

It was a dream come to for Rita. She fell in love with Paris from novels she read and always wanted to experience Paris, and now she was finally here.

"It's been so great to be away from home and not think about Bill and Barb," Mary Elle said, and Rita knew that she regretted even mentioning them by the look on her face.

"It's ok, Mary Elle. That's not something easy to forget or even deal with. You have been so brave and strong. I don't think I could've done that had it been Bob and I."

"This situation has put things into perspective for me. I don't want to continue living the way I lived before, Rita. I wasn't truly living. Come to think of it, I never really lived. My whole life revolved around Bill and the kids. Now, I can finally focus on what I want. How do I want to live?"

"You will, Mary Elle. This is not the end of your story. You have a long way to go, and I will be with you every step of the way," Rita said as she pulled her friend into a deep embrace.

"Thank you; I needed that," Mary Elle said as they pulled apart and continued on their way.

Time flew by, and soon it was lunchtime, and the ladies made their way to The Jules Verne.

"Mary Elle, you never mentioned we'd have lunch here! It's so beautiful!" Rita said in awe.

"I didn't want to spoil the surprise, Rita."

"Wow. Look at this view!" Rita said she didn't care about the people looking at her disapprovingly. She couldn't mask her excitement; She was in Paris, and no one would rain on her parade.

"It's amazing, isn't it?" Mary Elle asked as she wiped a tear away.

"It's better than I ever imagined. I can't wait to see the menu." Rita said, laughing as her stomach made an unexpected sound.

They took selfies with the Eiffel Tower in the background, and Mary Elle quickly sent them to her kids in the group chat before putting her phone away again. Lunch was unbelievable. How would they ever go back to their small town after this?

After lunch, the ladies went to The Champagne Bar to enjoy a flute of champagne. It wouldn't be a complete and fulfilling trip to Paris without enjoying some champagne. It was an incredible experience.

After the bar, they went to the souvenir shop and got some goodies for friends and family.

The evening arrived before they knew it, and the weather got a little chilly. Their first full day in Paris had been fantastic, and Rita was on cloud nine.

That night, the ladies opted to order dinner at their hotel to have a restful night. They were told to watch the Eiffel Tower from their balcony at midnight as a surprise.

"Rita, look!" Mary Elle called out to Rita.

Rita had been reading in the corner and eagerly joined Mary Elle on the balcony.

"That is so beautiful!" Rita said, placing a hand over her heart.

They stood there watching the Eiffel Tower lit up with twinkling lights.

THE NEXT DAY, they did a bike tour of Paris. Once again, they ultimately fell in love with the city. It was so much more than they ever expected or dreamed. They booked another tour for the following day, but this one was to see the outskirts of Paris. They saw cute little farmhouses and vineyards and sampled some wine and cheese. It was all delicious and relaxing. The weather was perfect, and the wine was exquisite. Mary Elle and Rita enjoyed themselves so much that they forgot to send photos and videos to their families. Then they saw immense fields of beautiful lavender. The smell was so relaxing and enchanting. They bought lavender soap, potpourri, tea, lotions, and sprays.

As their time in Paris progressed, Mary Elle thought less and less about her situation with Bill. She knew she had to let go of those awful thoughts and negative feelings to be present on this trip and enjoy it.

She realized that life continued, and she had to live her

life and love her life again. Mary Elle kept seeing signs with the phrases "Love the life you live" and "Love what you do." It was as if the universe wanted her to see that loving life, and what she did was necessary to live this life.

Mary Elle realized things wouldn't be the same once she was back home, but she had to choose what she would make of it. Bill had moved on, and she had to face that decision because pining around wouldn't be healthy for her.

On the third day, Rita and Mary Elle did a river cruise, which they enjoyed. On the last day of the trip, they visited Versailles and Moulin Rouge.

The days flew by, and they experienced so much. Mary Elle and Rita had so many tales to tell their families when they got home. They had been so busy they didn't have time to post much on social media, but enough to let their families know they arrived well and their daily activities. They started packing for their early flight back home. Bob would await them at the airport.

CHAPTER 8

Once home, Mary Elle stood in her large kitchen. It seemed incredibly empty now that she was back after her unforgettable trip with Rita.

She'd never felt lonelier in her own home, with no husband, no kids, not even a dog to keep her company—just her - alone with her thoughts. Rita had stayed over for three days, but she'd had to go back home to help Bill prep for a business trip.

Mary Elle walked around her home, a home that was once filled with so many happy memories and now seemed so cold and lonely. She tried to shake those negative thoughts from her mind, but she couldn't help it. She didn't feel like cooking anymore; it seemed pointless using this enormous kitchen to prepare a meal for one. She didn't want to go out to eat because then she had to make small talk, and she hated the pity that filled everyone's eyes now when they spoke to her.

Mary Elle grabbed her purse and keys and jumped into her car's driver's seat. She didn't know where she was going, but she knew she had to get out of that empty house. She got on the highway and headed north.

Mary Elle kept going until she saw a familiar exit and got off there. She hadn't thought about this place in a long time. She remembered cruising these streets with her parents during school breaks. Mary Elle had always enjoyed the small-town charm of Willow Heights. When her father passed away a few years ago, he'd left her at their vacation home.

Mary Elle hadn't been back here since she and Bill had gotten married. The house was empty and had been for the last few years.

She drove up to the house, and it was exactly as she remembered it. It was a white wooden house with a wraparound porch. She parked her car and made her way to the front door. She lifted the floor mat, and sure enough, the keys were there. Though the house had been empty, Mrs. Adelman, the next-door neighbor, watched over it.

Mary Elle looked around, impressed with how well the house had fared. A little dusty, but nothing a good cleaning couldn't fix. She felt strange standing in the place by herself. As she walked through every room, distinct memories came rushing in. Memories of time spent there with her family, memories of playing hide and seek with DeeAnn.

She felt a sense of peace wash over her she had not felt in a long time. It was only an hour and a half away from her current home, but it was far enough to escape everyone's pitying looks. Was she considering moving here? Her mind raced with the idea, and suddenly she felt hope for her future.

MARY ELLE HAD QUICKLY GOTTEN WRAPPED up in the excitement of her decision to move to Willow Heights that she'd forgotten the main reason she'd jumped in her car, to begin with, was to find some food.

Her stomach growled, and she decided it was time to head out and explore. She remembered seeing a street market on the square as she drove in. She glanced at the clock, surprised to see she'd been cleaning for two hours.

Mary Elle grabbed her keys and walked over to the town's square where the farmer's market was held. Mary Elle had always loved a good street market. She found them charming and hard to resist. She enjoyed supporting small businesses and had a soft spot for artisan candles, jewelry, and soaps.

"Would you like to try some cheese?" she heard someone say.

"I'd love to!" she headed over to the booth.

The young man sliced a piece of cheese and handed it over to her on a toothpick.

Mary Elle popped it in her mouth and said, "Oh my! That's the best cheese I've ever had!" she said.

The young man chuckled and handed her another piece. "It's a local favorite. We make it at our family farm," he said as he stretched out his hand. "I'm David Clarke from Willow Acres."

"Mary Elle," she said, shaking his hand.

"How long are you visiting us for?" he asked as he cut up some fruits and placed them in a small bowl for her. "We grow these over at the farm," he explained.

"Oh, I'm not visiting. I just moved here."

"Welcome to Willow Heights. I hope to see you over at Willow Acres once you've settled in," David said with a smile and helped other customers.

Mary Elle smiled and put some money in the tip jar as she made way for the newcomers. She had a smile on her face as she walked to the artisan candle booth.

. . .

Mary Elle was having a fantastic time at the street market. She bought a few lavender and honeysuckle soaps. She'd taste-tested so many jams–she didn't even know there were so many flavors. Oh, and the desserts were just divine. Mary Elle usually tried to stay away from sweets, but she deserved a treat after everything she'd been through recently. She'd be mindful next time and not give in to the temptation.

The people in Willow Heights were lovely. They were all very welcoming and, best of all, no one knew what was going on with Bill. She felt right at home and hadn't once thought about her situation back home. This was just the fresh start she needed.

The sun was setting, and she headed back to Helena Springs. She was sure now that she wanted to make a life for herself here in Willow Heights. She would make the needed arrangements to have electricity and running water at the house and come back as soon as possible. On her drive back home, she turned the music up, sang along, and dreamt of the life she wanted to have.

"Mom, are you sure you're ok?" Tiffany asked for what felt like the millionth time. Mary Elle wished there was a way to convince her daughter she was okay. She didn't want Tiffany worrying about her when she should focus on school and enjoying her last semester with friends.

"Honestly, honey, I'm fine."

"I'm coming over this weekend–so that we can spend some much-needed mother-daughter time."

Mary Elle knew that Tiffany's mind was not changing once she set her mind on something, so she didn't even try. The electricity and water at her future home should be up and running by the weekend. Mary Elle had told no one about her plans of moving to Willow Heights yet; maybe Tiffany coming over would be an opportunity for her to take her there and get Tiffany to stop worrying about her.

"Sounds lovely, honey. I'll be looking forward to it."

They spoke for a few more minutes as Tiffany filled her in on what she had been learning in school and her plans for after college. Mary Elle loved the excitement in Tiffany's voice as she spoke about her future. It had been a long time since Mary Elle had felt the same zest for life, but when she thought of Willow Heights, she felt an excitement that she had never felt before, and she couldn't wait to tell everyone the news.

"Oh, Mom, hold on. Melanie is calling me. I'll patch her in so we can 3-way." The line fell silent, and both her girls were on the line a few seconds later.

"How are you holding up, mom?" Melanie asked.

"I'm doing well, honey. How is the city treating you?"

"It's great," Melanie said, but her tone seemed off.

"Are you sure everything is okay?"

"Yes, mom. Don't worry about me. Why don't you visit? It would be nice to get away for a while and not deal with gossip."

"I wanted to wait a while before bringing this up. But I'm thinking of moving."

"Moving, where?" Tiffany asked.

"To Willow Heights."

Everett's shouting interrupted them, and Melanie quickly hung up the phone.

"What was that about?" Mary Elle asked Tiffany.

Tiffany sighed before explaining, "Mel says Everett has been on edge because he's working on a significant project. You know how he gets."

Tiffany had never been a fan of Everett and had told Melanie many times before she married him. Once they had gotten married, she'd kept her comments to herself out of respect for their relationship, but Mary Elle could tell that she still hadn't warmed up to him by her voice. She didn't blame her; he always came off as detached and self-centered.

Mary Elle hoped that he was different with Melanie in private, but she wasn't so sure. Melanie was so loving and giving that she needed someone to reciprocate that love.

"Mel says they're going to try for a baby again," Tiffany said, interrupting Mary Elle's thoughts.

"Oh, that's lovely," Mary Elle said, but her stomach knotted up. She would love to be a grandma and have a little grand-baby to dote on, but she hoped Melanie was not using this to save her marriage.

Mary Elle knew things were rocky between Melanie and Everett, and although Melanie had once believed he was her prince charming, he'd now become an ogre, which was clear to all of them. Things changed since Everett took in more jobs and had more responsibilities and clients to keep happy. Even during Christmas, he was away and didn't call Melanie, but she didn't dare intrude on Melanie's relationship. She knew that sometimes things weren't as they appeared, and she could have been mistaken about everything and didn't want to drive Melanie away.

But Mary Elle couldn't shake that feeling that they had rushed into this marriage. She remembered Mel mentioning that they disagreed on when and how to start their family. Melanie felt that her inner clock was ticking faster and time was running out, although she was still very young. Everett wanted a family down the road but agreed to disagree and let it happen when it would happen.

"Tell me more about your move, mom? Do you know where you will move to? Will it be near Auntie D?"

Mary Elle almost laughed at the mention of her sister. "Auntie D, Tiffany? Really? She and I have been practically

ABIGAIL BECK

strangers for so long that I barely remember what she looks like."

That was a lie. Mary Elle knew exactly what DeeAnn looked like. She spent many nights searching for her sister online and stalking her online profile, though she would never admit it to anyone.

"I'll never understand why you two are not close."

Mary Elle would never understand either. DeeAnn was younger than Mary Elle by five years, and when she was born, Dee was Mary Elle's world. She had always wanted a younger sister - when she found out her mother was pregnant, she had been ecstatic. Mary Elle would read her younger sister bedtime stories every night and sing her lullabies until she fell asleep.

All of that changed once Dee turned eleven. No one could explain why. It was a drastic change. Dee no longer wanted anything to do with Mary Elle and would often do things to hurt her. She even cut a bunch of her hair off once in the night.

Their parents said it was just a phase and that things would be back to normal soon enough, but as they got older, things just got worse. Mary Elle missed her sister and often replayed scenarios in her mind, hoping to figure out how things fell apart.

She kept tabs on her by checking her online profiles and knew that DeeAnn lived a few hours away in Savannah. DeeAnn was a teacher and loved to travel. She also dabbled in photography, but apart from the things she published online, Mary Elle knew little about her sister, breaking her heart.

CHAPTER 9

Melanie waited at the airport entrance for Everett. They were taking a weekend trip to visit her mom's new home. Mary Elle shared many of her childhood stories with her and her siblings about Willow Heights, but they had never visited. Visiting the town that held many of her mother's fondest childhood memories had always been on Melanie's bucket list.

She rechecked her watch. Everett was always running late; she had been reminding him all day to please be on time so they wouldn't miss their flights. He hated when she did that. He said she could be such a nag. She didn't enjoy nagging him, but he would get nothing done if she didn't.

Apart from his photography career, Everett cared little about anything else. He was rarely home, but it was still as if she was there alone when he was. Melanie watched as a pregnant woman exited a taxi with the help of her husband. She looked down at her flat stomach and felt a slight tug at her heart.

She and Everett had tried to have a baby early in their marriage but hadn't been able to. They hadn't been able to go to a doctor to see if there was a reason they couldn't have kids. Everyone made it seem effortless; surely, something was wrong with her? Maybe that was when things between them changed? Melanie would get checked out once they came back from visiting her mother. She hoped having a baby would draw them closer together. She missed the way things used to be when they first began dating.

Everett used to be very caring and affectionate. He loved spending time with her and would always invite her to his photoshoots; it was almost as if being apart from her was physically painful to him. Now, it was the complete opposite. She often felt like just being around her was a drag for him. She didn't know what had caused the drastic change in their relationship, but she would work to make things right again. Another reason she had planned the trip was to speak to Everett privately about planning a family again. He had been away working on projects for months, and discussing this over a phone or video call didn't feel right.

She was about to turn around and head inside to start the check-in process when a taxi pulled up in front of her. She looked up, and sure enough, her husband's annoyed but handsome face was staring back at her from inside the car. He quickly jumped out of the sedan and got his carry-on bag out of the vehicle.

"Hi, honey," she said.

"I'm here. I'm on time like I said I would be," Everett said as he walked past her.

Melanie did her best to catch up, but Everett was not in a good mood. He was speeding through the airport, not caring who he had to push out of his way.

By the time Melanie finally caught up to him, he was at the checkout counter. He was chatting up the woman at the counter and mindlessly extended his hand out for Melanie's boarding pass without glancing her way. The woman didn't notice Melanie either. Her eyes were for Everett only, and Melanie had never felt so invisible before in her life.

Once they finished checking in and going through TSA, they took a seat and waited for their flight to be called for boarding.

"How was your day?" Melanie asked once they were settled in

Everett groaned. "It was fine. It would have been better if I did not have to catch this flight. Not sure why I have to visit your mother. Now I'm going to fall behind on editing."

"Honey, I told you, mom invited us over, and I'm looking forward to seeing how she's settling in and where she'll be living. It is going to be a great trip. Plus, Tiffany and Ruby will be there too."

Everett sighed, put his earbuds in, pulled his laptop out, and started working.

Melanie sat back and let out a small sigh. This would be a long flight, she thought as she looked down at her stomach and quietly caressed it.

It hadn't been five minutes when Everett let out a long dramatic sigh, stood up, and announced he would buy something to eat.

"Could you get me some water, please?"

Everett stiffened at Melanie's request, and she instantly regretted asking him. She shut her eyes and took a deep breath, preparing herself for what was to come. Everett didn't make a scene, to her surprise, and she let out a sigh of relief.

It had only been two years of marriage, but it felt like a lifetime. Melanie tried to stay positive and convince herself that everything would work out, but being mistreated by Everett almost every day made it challenging to keep the faith.

ABIGAIL BECK

* * *

Mary Elle sat in her front porch rocking chair, waiting for the girls and Everett to arrive. She was looking forward to showing them around Willow Heights. It wasn't too far from Atlanta, only a couple of hours north depending on traffic, tucked away in the Georgia mountains, but it felt completely different. Life here was simple and slow-paced compared to Helena Springs.

When she inherited the house, she also inherited all the furniture; she was grateful for that because apart from activating the water and electrical account again, all she had to do was clean and put out fresh linens to move in.

Mary Elle felt silly for being nervous about having the girls visit; she didn't know what they would think about her moving here or how she was handling the situation with their dad. She didn't care about what people back home thought about her. The older she got, the more she understood it was okay to live a life others did not understand. Her life was her own, and now that she didn't have to worry about Bill's image or his idea of what their life should be like–she could live the way she saw fit.

Mary Elle wasn't sure if she was handling things the right way. What were you supposed to do when your husband leaves you? Are you supposed to drown yourself in your sorrows? Brush your shoulders off and move on? She had already cried her eyes out. Mary Elle had been angry and hurt, but now she was ready to start her life over. She and Bill had shared a beautiful life, and without him, she wouldn't have her kids. Because of that, she could never hate him or wish him a hard life. She would always cherish all the years they had spent together and hold those memories close to her heart.

However, she looked forward to moving past the pain

and embarrassment. It was time for her to move on and make a life for herself. It was time for her to dream again. She refused to let the pain and betrayal plague her.

A red sedan pulled into her front yard, and Tiffany and Melanie quickly jumped out of the car and ran over to her. "Mom! This house is so cute," Tiffany said as she threw her arms around her.

Tiffany made way for Melanie to hug her mom and made her way inside to check out the rest of the house.

"Everett, it's great to see you. It's been too long." Mary Elle said when she spotted her son-in-law. He looked like he had just woken up from a nap. He muttered something under his breath and walked into the house.

"How have you been, mom?" Melanie asked, trying to distract them from her husband's rude behavior.

"I'm great, honey. So happy to have you all here. How are you? How's Everett?"

"Oh, he's fine, mom. He's under a deadline, so he's a little grumpy, but he'll be fine once this project is over."

Mary Elle had heard this before, and she was wondering if Melanie realized how often she used that line to excuse her husband's behavior. Mary Elle didn't want to meddle in their relationship, but she worried for Melanie, and she didn't want her daughter to be stuck in a loveless marriage.

However, she didn't want to project her insecurities into her kids. Just because her marriage had ended, it didn't mean Melanie's marriage was on the rocks. Perhaps Everett had just been having a rough time. Mary Elle gave Everett the benefit of the doubt, and she would trust her daughter to make the right choices in her own life. She would not ruin the trip by imagining things and worrying. Her girls were here, and it was time to focus on them and show them the wonders of Willow Heights.

She hoped that they would love Willow Heights as much

as she did after this trip, and together, they would make some unforgettable memories. She had always wanted to bring them here, but they could not go on family trips because of Bill's work schedule.

Looking back now, that would always be one of her biggest regrets. She had always felt a bit of jealousy towards families that went on family trips and posted the photos all over social media. As a child, she had always dreamt of one day coming to Willow Heights with her own family and creating many memories. Willow Heights also had a great campsite with many outdoor activities. She looked forward to planning a trip there with the kids sometime soon and brought it up once everyone had settled in and were chatting around the table, enjoying tea and freshly baked cookies.

"Camping?" Tiffany repeated, scrunching her nose up.

"Oh, don't be like that, Tiff. It might be fun!" Melanie said.

"Or we might get eaten by a bear," Tiffany replied sarcastically.

"I'm sure there are no bears there. It's more like a camping resort." Melanie said with a wry smile on her face. Mary Elle had forgotten how un-outdoorsy her kids were.

"It would be good to be out in nature and disconnect from the hustle and bustle of the city life. Reconnecting with nature is also important and healthy," Melanie added.

"Well, okay, I guess we could try. But after that, we are going on a spa weekend!" Tiffany said.

"Oh, this is so exciting. I am sure Everett will love to go with us. We need to invite Michael as well!" Melanie said, and Mary Elle broke into a smile.

Maybe this was just what they all needed. She hadn't seen Melanie smiling so brightly in a long time. Tiffany still didn't seem too keen on the idea, but she was being a good sport and sat back quietly, smiling as she watched her mother and sister begin planning. Mary Elle knew Tiffany might not be much of a camper, but she would do anything to see her family happy.

* * *

THE FOLLOWING DAY, Tiffany woke up to the smell of bacon and pancakes. Her stomach grumbled, and she quickly jumped out of bed, made a quick trip to the restroom, and headed downstairs, admiring the photo gallery on her way down.

The wall was full of photos of her mother, grandparents, and aunt DeeAnn. Tiffany loved her aunt Dee and hated that she and her mother weren't close. Even though Mary Elle and her sister didn't have a close-knit relationship, DeeAnn always tried to stay in touch with her nieces and nephew.

"Good morning!" she said, sitting at the kitchen island.

"Good morning, Sweetie! How did you sleep?"

"Like a baby. I knocked out as soon as my head hit the pillow."

Mary Elle smiled and placed a fruit bowl in the island's center. Followed by a serving plate stacked with pancakes and another with bacon and sausages. Tiffany helped her mom take everything over to the dining room. Once they finished setting up, Melanie appeared.

"Are we having guests?"

Mary Elle laughed, "I might have gotten carried away while cooking."

"It looks amazing and smells divine, Mom," Melanie said as she placed a quick kiss on her mother's cheek and found a seat at the table.

"Is Everett joining us?"

"He's still sleeping. He went to sleep late working on that project."

"We'll save him a plate then." Mary Elle said as she sat down and joined her daughters.

The women enjoyed their breakfast as they sat around catching up, and Tiffany filled them in on her latest boyfriend. One of her classmates and coworkers at the restaurant she worked part-time in while at college.

"He's not my boyfriend. We just hang out and enjoy each other's company," she explained. Tiffany didn't have many boyfriends growing up.

She had gone on dates here and there, but none of them ever stuck. From a young age, Tiffany had promised herself that she would never lose sight of her dreams and put a man before them the way her mother had. She never voiced it aloud, but she'd known for a long time that her mom wasn't living the life she had always dreamed of.

One day, she'd come home early from soccer practice when she'd overheard her parents talking in the kitchen. Her mother told her dad how she wanted to start a party planning business. She seemed so happy and excited and laid out a very thought-out business plan to him, but her dad had quickly shut her down, and Mary Elle never spoke of it again. It was then that Tiffany swore to herself that she would focus on her personal goals and only then think about having a husband or kids.

MELANIE'S STOMACH WAS FULL, but more importantly, so was her heart. She hadn't realized how much she missed spending time with her mother and sister until now. It was almost as if a piece of her had been missing. Sure, they spoke on the phone often, and video chatted a few times a week, but it was not the same as being face to face with them.

She only hoped that Everett would come around. It upset

him to have missed a deadline for a project, which he blamed Melanie for. He thought he had another week to work on it, but it was due yesterday. Everett could get a two-day extension, but that meant he would be in a mood for the rest of the trip, and he blamed her for missing his deadline. She wasn't sure how the blame fell on her when he'd written the date wrong in his planner, but she said nothing in fear of making matters worse.

The romantic weekend she'd planned would not be happening. He would fly out a few hours after they landed back home to make matters worse. The baby talk would have to wait yet again.

"I thought we could check out a few shops around town and have lunch at Willow Acres." Mary Elle said, cutting into Melanie's thoughts.

"Oh, do you think we could visit a couple of thrift stores?" Tiffany asked. Her graduation was a few months away, and as a graduation present, her father had given her the money she would use to rent an apartment. She hadn't found a place yet, but she was using the money from her job at the restaurant to find decorative pieces and small Knickknacks.

"Of course!" Mary Elle said as she grabbed her purse and keys.

Melanie stopped at the bottom of the staircase on their way out as she overheard her mother and sister talking. She wondered if she should tell Everett they were leaving or take him a plate of food upstairs, but she decided not to interrupt him and sour his mood.

She sent him a quick text letting him know they were leaving and had left food for him downstairs. Melanie smiled as she heard her mom and sister talking about Tiffany's plan for her apartment and the items she hoped to find today. Her sister came alive when she spoke about it. It was hard not to get excited with her. She loved the way things seemed to be unfolding for her sister and mother.

Everyone expected her mother to fall apart after her father left her for Barbara, but now her mother seemed happier. It almost felt like her mom had been holding back all these years and would only now finally start living.

* * *

As they walked to Main Street, they took in the change in pace. Tiffany felt like it transported her back in time. Willow Heights is precisely what you would expect from a small town in America.

Growing up just outside of Atlanta, Tiffany was elated to be here. She was sure she wanted to offer this experience to her future customers when they booked to stay in her B&B. It was still a few years before she could run her own place, but a girl could dream.

She loved how everyone in Willow Heights was friendly, not fake nice, but genuine, something you didn't experience in big cities. When someone asked how you were doing, they stopped to listen to your response; they didn't just continue walking away. It was something so small, but she appreciated it. She also loved the look and feel of all the businesses in town. It felt like a time warp of sorts. She especially loved the old Candy Shop. They offered saltwater taffy and other classics, and, best of all, it was all made by the locals.

Tiffany loved walking along the square. There were many shops with eye-catching window displays. She could only imagine what Christmas would be like here.

There were also lots of floral and fruit trees adorning the streets. They had benches to sit on, and people watch. Tiffany could see why her mother would pick Willow Heights to move to. There was a peace you could feel. People took their time and enjoyed their days. There was no rush hour traffic to beat, no road rage, and you could walk to get anything you needed. The birds were chirping, and the flowers were blooming. The perfect day to be out exploring with her two most favorite people.

Tiffany and Mary Elle both noticed Melanie's sad look. They knew things between her and Everett weren't that great right now. They didn't want to pry, but they were both concerned about Melanie.

"Melanie, is everything ok?" Mary Elle asked.

"Yes, I'm sad that Everett will have to leave early."

"You can leave early too if you need to," Mary Elle said.

"No, it's ok; I'll just be home alone since Everett will return to work. They changed some of his deadline dates, and he's now having to work faster to meet them."

Tiffany knew that there was more to this story than Melanie told them, but she didn't push for any additional information. It might be selfish, but she wanted to enjoy her time with her mother and sister. They should focus on the present moment. Melanie's marriage might bring up old memories and wounds for her mom, bringing her down. She made a mental note to carve out some time to talk to her sister alone before their trip was over.

"It's ok, honey, soon this project will be over, and you'll have time together again," she overheard her mother say.

"Hey, maybe we should head out to the farm. Ruby said she would meet us there for lunch?" Tiffany asked, maybe speaking a bit too loudly.

Mary Elle looked at her wristwatch and, with a laugh, said, "Wow, time got away from us while shopping, didn't it?"

"Let's go. I cannot wait to hear about Ruby's new job. When we last spoke, she seemed excited on the phone," Melanie said.

Tiffany smiled, glad they had diverted their attention from a glum topic to one more optimistic.

RUBY WAS ALREADY SEATED at the restaurant when they arrived at Willow Acres. Tiffany had never seen such a beautiful place. Not in person anyway, but she had seen similar locations in many movies.

Large beautiful trees and flowers stretched out on either side of the long driveway towards the farm. At the end of the driveway, there was a beautiful white house. They held wedding receptions and other events there.

The restaurant was on the far right of the house. It looked like a greenhouse; They constructed the walls and roof out of glass, and there were endless amounts of plants used to decorate the space. It was truly breathtaking.

"You're here!" Ruby exclaimed as she got up from her seat and hugged them.

"I've missed you so much!" Tiffany said as she hugged her back.

"I've missed you all," Ruby said as they took their seats at the table.

A young man appeared and introduced himself as Wyatt, their server, and handed out menus while taking their drink order.

"This place is so beautiful," Melanie said as she looked around.

"It is. I can't believe we've never been to Willow Heights before." Tiffany said,

"I have to admit, when I heard you were moving to a tiny town in the middle of nowhere, I worried a lot about you. However, I am so glad you invited us over and that we are getting to see what it is like here. It is so beautiful, mom. I can see why you want to call this your home, and now I can say I fully support your decision." Melanie said to her mother as she rested her hand on hers.

"It makes me so happy to hear that. I would never want to worry you girls about me. I want you to know you all are always welcome to visit." Mary Elle said with happy tears in her eyes.

Tiffany smiled as she watched her mother, Melanie, and Ruby interacting. She hadn't realized how worried her mom had been about her life choices and their concerns.

She was glad they had cleared that out of the way and that her mom could now focus on settling in and making a life for herself. Tiffany had spoken to her dad, and she knew he had already moved in with Barbara and was genuinely happy. She wanted the same for her mother. Sure, the family dynamic would be different, but when it came down to it, they were family, no matter what.

"So, tell us about your job?" Melanie said to Ruby, shifting Tiffany's attention from her thoughts.

"Yes! I am so excited for you. I know how hard you've been trying to find an opening in your field." Tiffany said, but it bewildered her to see Ruby's face go sullen.

Ruby had graduated a few months ago with a degree in finance. She hadn't been able to find a job until she signed up with a staffing agency.

"Yeah, about that… I don't think I'll be taking the job." Ruby said,

"Why? What happened?" Melanie asked.

Ruby stared down at the table, fidgeting with her fingers, finding it hard to make eye contact.

"The job is at Bill's firm, and with everything that has gone on, it doesn't feel right."

"Oh, Honey, please don't turn the job down on my accord. You worked hard on your studies, and you deserve it. Nothing would make me happier than seeing you succeed in

ABIGAIL BECK

your career path. Bills company is a great company. I know it's difficult to get a job at his company which proves that this job is meant for you."

Bill's company was one of the most well-known commercial development firms. They rarely had new openings because once people worked there, they stayed there. The work environment was great, and they also had excellent benefits.

Ruby looked up and blinked away the tears that had formed in her eyes. "Do you mean that?" She asked Mary Elle.

"Of course!" Mary Elle said as a man approached their table with their drinks.

He handed them their drinks and introduced himself as Thomas Clarke, the Owner of Willow Acres.

"Is this your first time here?" he asked with a gentle smile.

"Our mom just moved to Willow Heights, and we are doing some exploring," Melanie responded.

"I see. I hope you are enjoying your visit. Willow Heights is a wonderful place to live. I am sure you will feel right at home in no time."

"This place is like a dream. Mom used to spend her summers here while growing up, and I can't believe this is our first time visiting." Tiffany said as she marveled at the simplistic beauty of this quaint town.

"Once you're done with your meal, I would love to show you around the farm. It's been a while since we've had any newcomers."

"That would be wonderful, Mr. Clarke." Mary Elle said.

"Please call me, Thomas. I will get out of your way now. Someone will be out shortly to take your food order," he said as he bowed his head and walked away.

The women enjoyed their lunch. It was fresh and delicious. As promised, Thomas showed them around the property when they finished their meal.

"It's so nice to have fresh faces around here. Willow Heights used to be a tourist destination. We've been struggling to get newcomers for a while." Thomas said as they stood near a sunflower field.

"Why is that?" Tiffany asked, not understanding why anyone would not want to visit this place.

"I guess there's not much going on here to bring in a crowd," Thomas said as his face fell and his eyes filled with dark shadows.

"But this place is beautiful! I can see families coming here for vacation. It just needs a bit of marketing and getting the word out." Melanie said. Thomas smiled sadly, not understanding what Melanie meant by marketing.

"This here is my nephew, David," Thomas said, gesturing to a young man that approached them.

"I remember you from the Farmers Market," Mary Elle said as he came closer.

"That's right. I am so glad you visited Willow Acres."

"These are my daughters, Melanie and Tiffany," Mary Elle said, gesturing to the girls, "and our family friend, Ruby."

"Pleased to meet you all. I'd shake your hands, but...." David said, holding his paint-filled hands, "I've been painting all day. We're trying to get Willow Acres back to its glory days."

"It is a beautiful property." Mary Elle said,

"That it is, but unfortunately, the business has been extremely slow. We are trying to think of ways to bring in the crowds. We gave it a bit of a face-lift, and I put out an ad for an event planner but have gotten no bites yet."

"Oh, don't worry about that. I know just the person for the job." Tiffany said, with a glimmer in her eyes. She knew she was treading on dangerous territory here, but it was worth a shot. Everyone turned to look at her in anticipation.

"My mother, of course! No one throws a party like Mary Elle Sloane!" she said, using her mother's maiden name.

Tiffany felt her mother stiffen next to her, and she wondered if she should have kept her mouth shut. She knew it caught Mary Elle entirely off guard, and she didn't mean to put her on the spot.

"Is that so?" David asked with a bemused smile.

"I love to plan events, but I don't have any professional experience." Mary Elle said as she shifted uncomfortably.

"She's being modest. She truly is the best at what she does. Back home, they talked about her parties for months." Melanie said, smiling proudly, and Tiffany nodded in agreement, thinking back to all the beautiful memories her mother had created.

Ruby joined in and said, "She always handled all our school events; Prom, Homecoming, Graduation, all beautifully crafted by Mary Elle."

"It wouldn't hurt to try her, would it?" Thomas, who had been standing quietly nearby, asked David.

"It'd be great to have you onboard," David said with a genuine smile on his face.

"Don't you need to interview me first? Call up some references?" Mary Elle asked.

"We do things differently here at Willow Acres," Thomas said with a shrug and a glint in his eyes.

"Wow, I was not expecting this, but I'd love to try it!" Mary Elle said, and Tiffany felt her shoulders relax. She was worried that this would be much too soon for her mother.

The girls all squealed in delight as they enveloped Mary Elle in a hug.

* * *

ONCE BACK HOME, Mary Elle reflected on how quickly her life was changing. Things were working out so perfectly. She would have laughed if you had told her a few months ago that her marriage would end abruptly and she'd move to her childhood vacation home. If you'd told her last week that she would fit right in and land a job doing what she's always dreamed of doing, she would've thought you'd gone mad.

Rita always told Mary Elle that life would hand you precisely what you needed when you opened yourself up to life. Maybe Rita was right all along. She had been comfortable in her life before. Now, she felt like she was finally living and saying yes to life again. She was excited about all the new possibilities that had opened up for her.

Mary Elle and the girls planned the camping trip, and Tiffany and Melanie gave her mom some advertising ideas to help Thomas out. They wanted Mary Elle to succeed in her new job and make a good impression on everyone.

They loved that Mary Elle was moving on in life, making new friends, and even starting a new career. The girls felt comfortable knowing where Mary Elle would work and what route she would take to get to work. They met her boss, Thomas. He seemed like a lovely guy with lots of patience. They met David, who was very amicable and kind. This little town was beautiful and safe. They also started planning future visits to Willow Heights. With summer quickly approaching, they couldn't wait to see all the outdoor events the town would offer.

The weekend flew by, and the girls were getting ready to fly back home and go back to their work and school routines. Mary Elle worried about Melanie and saw lots of red flags but didn't dare say anything to her because she'd learned from her personal experiences that sometimes things aren't as they appear. Things need to be worked out by those in the relationship and not outsiders.

CHAPTER 10

On Sunday night, Mary Elle was preparing to start her new job the following day. She was not sure of what to wear. It was a laid-back atmosphere, but she wanted to look professional on her first day. She was laying out her outfit when the phone rang. It was Rita.

"Hey Mary Elle, just got news you have a new job?" Rita asked.

"Yes, I start tomorrow. I'll be the one planning parties, receptions, and any other events," Mary Elle said.

"Wow, that's amazing! What is your boss like?"

"His name is Thomas, and he seems very nice," Mary Elle said while putting away some clothes.

"Is he good-looking?" Rita asked bluntly.

"Yes! He is very handsome, but he is my boss." Mary Elle said, blushing, even though Rita couldn't see her.

She wasn't going to lie, and she wasn't blind either. He was a handsome man. He looked nothing like Bill.

Bill was tall and slender. While Thomas was very fit from working at the farm his whole life. Thomas was a manly man and had beautiful, gentle green eyes that shined with pride every time he spoke of the farm.

"Did you see a ring on his finger?" Rita asked.

Mary Elle laughed and said, "Rita, don't be so silly."

"I have a good feeling about this, Mary Elle; things are speeding up and changing for the better!"

"We're planning a camping trip with the kids. Will you and Robert be joining us?" Mary Elle asked Rita, knowing that Rita was not an outdoorsy person.

"I'll have to ask Robert if he can take those days off work," Rita said skeptically.

"Oh, ok, let me know. We can also plan a weekend for you to visit Willow Heights."

"Yes, I would love to go by this weekend. Robert won't come along, though. He is flying out to Seattle."

"I'll have your room ready," Mary Elle said cheerfully. Mary Elle loved to host friends and family. She had already come up with a list of ideas for fun meals and activities she wanted to do with Rita once she visited.

* * *

Mary Elle woke up early on Monday morning and got ready for work. She felt like she had come a long way since she and Bill separated. Sometimes she felt overwhelmed, and she shed a tear here and there, but the heartache was not as bad as before.

The one thing she missed the most was having someone she knew had her back. Mary Elle realized that their relationship had not been a romantic one for some time. They were more like old friends; they also hadn't been intimate with each other for some time now.

She hadn't spoken to Bill, but she no longer felt anger

towards him. She knew he could have done things differently, but she could finally see that this was for the best.

MARY ELLE WORE black slacks and a silk floral button-down blouse. She blow-dried her hair and curled the ends just like she liked it. She was excited to see what the day would bring. What new people she would meet, and who her first clients would be.

She got a warm fuzzy feeling just driving up to the farmhouse. It was all so beautiful and inviting. As she got closer, her nerves started acting up. She had never had an actual job before, and she didn't want to let anyone down. She sat in her car for a few minutes, taking deep breaths, before venturing into the office.

Once in the main office, she met with Thomas. He was a morning person and was already up and getting things going. He smiled brightly when he noticed Mary Elle come in. "Good morning; great to see you."

"Thanks for having me." Mary Elle said shyly. She had never been shy before, but she felt out of place and questioned her decision to take this job right now.

"Let me show you to your office," Thomas said as he walked towards two double doors on the far right.

The office had two large bay windows; one faced the lake, and the other faced a lush forest. The office was very cozy. She had a desk and desktop computer with some catalogs for ideas and businesses they used in previous events for flowers and decorations.

Mary Elle was great at doing DIYs as well. She loved being creative and creating with her hands. As you can imagine, she had millions of new ideas about how to decorate her new office. She and the girls had come up with many great ideas for promoting the restaurant, farmhouse, and event planning services.

She thought of calling up Rita to see if she had any invitations or programs from her previous events that she had planned; she would also look for pictures to make a collage for a flyer showcasing her work and a portfolio on hand to show potential clients her ideas.

"How do you like your new office, Mary Elle?" Thomas asked as she was daydreaming.

"Oh, sorry, I was thinking about how to decorate it. I love it."

"It's alright; I saw your smile and knew you were creating things in your mind," he said.

"Are there any annual events that you provide services for?" Mary Elle asked, eager to plan.

"Yes, we host several. Since summer is right around the corner, Willow Heights will start hosting their summer camp here. We rent out the cabins in the South of the farm, and we provide meals for their campers. The locals love sending their kids to camp here because they know the camp counselors, and it brings back fond memories of their own camping experiences." Thomas explained.

It elated Mary Elle to be a part of this organization. She thought of other events they could host to showcase their event planning services and bring tourists. She was also thinking about who she could invite from her friends to come and vacation here. Who wouldn't want to come and relax here, especially with all this lush beauty and nature around?

THOMAS SHOWED Mary Elle around the rest of the farm and gave her keys to her very own golf cart to get around the property. They also went over her schedule and benefits. The

Farm was even more significant than she had imagined. She hoped she wouldn't get lost. Mary Elle enjoyed her time with Thomas. He loved Willow Acres, which is evident in how his face lit up every time he spoke about it.

"My great grandad first founded Willow Acres," Thomas said as they walked around the cabins where the summer camp kids would be staying. Mary Elle made mental notes of things she would like to get fixed before the kids arrived.

"His family was impoverished and didn't have the funds to send him to any summer camps. He founded Willow Acres hoping to make it affordable for all kids to have a fun, safe place for summer," Thomas continued.

"Wow, that was very thoughtful of him. Do the kids stay here for free?"

"No, we offer scholarships that cover the camp cost for low-income households,"

"Is the scholarship money raised by the fundraisers we'll be hosting?" Mary Elle asked.

"Yes, and we'll be counting on you to develop some bright new ideas," Thomas said with a sparkle in his eye.

Mary Elle loved a challenge, and knowing that the money raised would help the kids only made her want to work that much harder.

As she watched Thomas speak about Willow Acres, she couldn't help but smile. His knowledge and excitement about the land and the town were a joy to observe. From what she had gathered in her short time in Willow Heights, everyone who lived here took great pride in their town.

She hadn't been here for very long, but this place felt like home. She had never felt like she belonged anywhere else the way she felt she belonged here.

* * *

"It's not that I don't enjoy having you around, but don't you think it's time you started heading home?" Thomas said as he leaned in the doorway of Mary Elle's office.

Mary Elle glanced at the time on her desktop computer, which showed twenty minutes past five.

"Oh wow. Time flew by today," she said with a laugh.

She gathered her things and prepared to leave the office. Mary Elle couldn't wait to call Rita and tell her all about her first day at work. She had noticed that she had overdressed today, and she would wear jeans with a nice button-down shirt and strappy sandals tomorrow.

She headed over to the main office to clock out for the day. David and Thomas were sitting at a desk discussing the barn remodel when she walked in. Both men sat up as they saw her.

"How was your first day?" David asked.

"It was wonderful. I have so many ideas that I'd love to run by you later this week."

"Sounds good. I'm happy you're a part of our team now. Sorry, I was not around much. I was a little busy remodeling one of the barns. I hope Uncle Thomas didn't bore you too much," David said with an evil laugh.

"Don't mind him; he likes to think he's funny," Thomas said as he gathered his things.

David hadn't been around much today, but she noticed the two constantly sharing friendly banter the few times she had seen him.

CHAPTER 11

In the basement, Mary Elle found old family photos that she didn't realize were there. Her favorite photographs were always the ones taken candidly. Going through the pictures, she felt a tug at her heart when she realized just how much she missed her sister.

She loved living here, but she was constantly flooded with childhood memories. Those memories only made her miss her sister more. Mary Elle remembered holidays spent here with her parents and DeeAnn. Her parents had passed away, but she cherished those moments now more than ever.

She looked back at what had gone wrong with DeeAnn. She wondered if she could reach out to her and rekindle their relationship somehow. It would be lovely to have her over and spend some time together. The house wasn't as big as her family's home, but it had everything and more than what one person needed.

Without even a second thought, she reached for her phone and sent her sister a quick message. She hoped her sister would answer and that they would salvage their relationship.

DeeAnn took some time to write back, but the wait was worth it for Mary Elle.

"Hi, how are you?" DeeAnn's message read.

"Great, how are you?" Mary Elle replied, with her heart racing.

"I've been super busy finishing up the school year. Can't wait for summer break."

"That's great. I meant to tell you I moved back to our old vacation house in Willow Heights. Maybe you could visit?" Mary Elle braced herself. She hoped her sister would jump at the invitation, but a part of her knew it wouldn't be so easy.

"I'm not sure I can. I'll be starting a part-time job this summer since the school's out,"

"Okay, whenever you get a little break, my doors open for you," Mary Elle said, feeling a little downhearted.

"I'll have to get back to you, Mary Elle. Have to go. I need to finish grading. Have a great night."

Mary Elle found solace because DeeAnn was willing to message her, and maybe there would be a reunion down the road for them to bury the hatchet.

* * *

MARY ELLE STUDIED the divorce papers they had served her a couple of days ago. She had signed them the same day she received them, but she was still unsettled. Mary Elle knew divorcing Bill was what needed to be done, but why did it feel so easy?

She and Bill had been married for so long, yet it felt like it had all meant nothing. Just a little signature, and everything would be erased.

"Penny, for your thoughts?" Thomas asked from the doorway to Mary Elle's office.

"Oh, sorry, were you standing there for long?"

"You seemed lost in thought, and I wasn't sure if I should interrupt. Is everything okay?"

"Yeah, everything is fine. It's just that I thought this whole divorce thing would be much more complicated."

"Ah, I see."

"I expected my husband to put up a fight and not be so cooperative." She hated to admit it, but she wished Bill would put up more of a fight. Instead, she felt like - he couldn't wait to get this over with so he could move on and leave her out in the cold.

"Is it a bad thing that he's not acting out?"

"No, of course not. It is just surprising. I guess I'll be a free woman in a shorter time than I imagined." Mary Elle laughed, "Now that the shock has worn out and I can reflect on the past - I realize we were more roommates than anything else, so this is definitely for the best."

"Lucky for you, Willow Heights is just the place for fresh starts."

"I'm beginning to believe you."

"Do you have a moment? I want to show you something."

"Right now? I'm kind of on the clock. I'm not sure what my boss will say."

"I know the old grump. I promise I'll put in a good word for you if he says anything," Thomas said with a gleam in his eyes.

"Okay then, if you insist."

MARY ELLE STARED out into the vast greatness of the mountains before her. Thomas had packed a small picnic from the pre-made sandwiches at the farm's gift shop and said he was taking her to his favorite spot in Willow Acres.

He mentioned that he often came here when he felt overwhelmed and needed a place to think. It was an overlook of the mountains. Being out in nature never ceased to amaze her. She felt so insignificant compared to the mountains.

"It's beautiful, isn't it?" Thomas said as he studied her.

"It's breathtaking."

"I can't imagine what you're feeling now. You've gone through a big life change with your marriage ending and starting your life over from zero." Thomas said as he sat down at a bench with a better view of the mountains and motioned for Mary Elle to sit next to him. "I know it's tough. It was tough for me, and I wasn't married nearly as long as you were. But I learned God uses every season of our lives to prepare us for what is coming. Like these leaves around us will change, and a new season will begin, so will your life change. Right now, you're simply preparing for a new season, and I do not doubt that the best is yet to come over your life."

"When did you become so wise, Mr. Clarke?" Mary Elle said as she bumped her shoulder into his.

Thomas didn't say anything. He smiled back, then sat back and enjoyed the view. This small adventure with Thomas was just what Mary Elle needed. She felt he understood her and wanted to show her there was more on the other side of this dark period. Mary Elle appreciated his gesture and sat back to enjoy the view and the companionship.

* * *

MARY ELLE SAT out on the deck, reading a new cozy mystery. The day was too lovely to be spent indoors. Rita had canceled her plans to visit this weekend because Bob hadn't been feeling well and had to cancel his business trip to Seattle. Mary Elle was wholly absorbed in her cozy mystery that

ABIGAIL BECK

when she heard someone yell out her name, it startled her, and she let out a small yelp.

"Mary Elle, come join us!" She looked up and spotted Dean waving her over. He was on a boat accompanied by the rest of the Willow Acres staff, including Thomas. She quickly set her book down and jogged to the end of her dock, where David was pulling the boat into.

"Welcome to the Willow Acres Initiation," Dean called out as the group broke out in giggles.

"We should have warned you that the guys randomly show up at our homes and kidnap us," Bailey said as she made space for Mary Elle to sit.

"Here, I thought I would have a boring day of lounging around," Mary Elle said with a laugh.

"No boring days allowed in Willow Heights!" Thomas called out from across the boat. Their eyes met, and they shared a smile that made Mary Elle blush.

Once they found a spot on the lake that they liked, Dean announced he had prepared an exquisite pizza menu for them to enjoy.

The first pizza was a fresh fruit salad pizza. It had a watermelon crust with cream cheese and colorful fruit pieces sprinkled on top. He also made mini brunch pizzas with butternut squash, kale, pomegranates, and goat cheese. He had prepared a blackberry Brie pizza on cinnamon focaccia for dessert.

"Ugh, Dean, let's get married already!" Patricia said, and Dean's cheeks instantly turned pink. Mary Elle had noticed that Patty enjoyed putting Dean on the spot. She wasn't sure if it was friendly banter or something else.

As everyone devoured Dean's creations, Thomas found his way to Mary Elle. "I hope you don't mind that we showed up unannounced," he said, sitting next to her.

"Not at all. I would have a boring Sunday if you all didn't show up."

"I don't know; you seemed pretty engrossed in that book."

"Read a book or spend some time with you and my favorite people in Willow Heights?" Mary Elle said with a pensive look and moving her hands, weighing the options.

"Hey! I'm hurt." Thomas said, placing his hand over his heart.

"Why?"

"Why am I not a part of your favorite people in Willow Heights group?"

Mary Elle laughed. "You're the leader of that group."

They smiled at each other, and their eyes locked. Mary Elle felt a rush of excitement inside her, and she glanced away.

The more time she spent with Thomas, the more she let her guard down. He was her first friend in Willow Heights, although sometimes she felt like something more could be between them.

Mary Elle sat back and closed her eyes. She loved the way the sun warmed her skin. Never in a million years would she ever dream that life could change and bring about so many fresh adventures and friendships in her life.

The heartache that had brought her out here seemed like a distant memory. She was so grateful to be working with such a fantastic group of people that made work fun and exciting.

Even her children were more in contact with her now. The emptiness she felt was slowly drifting away. She was also rediscovering herself. She had tapped into her creativity and was painting again and creating beautiful moments of celebration and happiness for others; that brought her immense satisfaction.

CHAPTER 12

It had been a few weeks since Mary Elle joined the Willow Acres team, and she was feeling like she was getting the hang of things.

Today would be a big test for her and her capabilities. She found herself in the middle of her office, checking her list for the 100th time. She kept trying to think of any little thing she might have missed, but nothing came to mind.

About three weeks ago, a young couple looking for a wedding venue approached them. The team had been ecstatic about the opportunity until they learned the couple was in a hurry, and it didn't leave them much time. They also had a very tight budget.

Mary Elle felt a great weight on her shoulders. She wanted to give the couple the wedding of their dreams, and she hoped they would recommend Willow Acres to their families and friends for future events. A lot was riding on the outcome of this event.

"How's it going?" Thomas asked, popping his head into Mary Elle's office

"According to my list, we're ready, but I can't help but feel like something is missing." She said as she paced back and forth in her office, unable to stay still.

"Hey, come here," Thomas said, placing his hands on her shoulders, "This wedding will go off without a hitch. I have seen the way you have meticulously handled everything. You're going to do great."

"I hope you're right because this is a tremendous deal for the farm and the town. Many people are counting on us."

"You said that right: us. You are not in this alone. Take a deep breath and remember we're a team now."

Mary Elle felt her shoulders relax. Thomas was right. They were a team, and they made a great team. She knew David, Jasper, Lisa, Patty, and the rest of the group would give it their all. They were a family here, and they were all rooting for the same team.

*   *   *

THE WEDDING WENT off without a hitch, as Thomas had predicted. Everyone loved the food and the venue. Mary Elle tried to stay out of the guests' way by standing near the back, observing everything.

The night had been exhausting but exciting, just the same. She had overheard many guests comment on how beautiful the venue was. They received many compliments on the décor and floral arrangements that Patty and Mary Elle worked on staying within the couple's budget.

The best compliment Mary Elle received was from the bride. Her eyes had welled up in tears as soon as she had walked into the venue the morning of the wedding.

She made her way around the venue, pointing out different things, and mentioned how she could not believe this was the same place she had seen the first time they had been there.

"Is this what you'd imagined?" her groom had asked her.

"No, this is better than I could've ever imagined!" she hugged Mary Elle. "Thank you so much. I don't know what we would've done without you."

As the couple had made their way around the venue, checking everything out, Mary Elle and Thomas stayed behind to give them privacy. Together, they admired the team's creation. Mary Elle was proud of the work they had done. They had had little time or funds, but they had created something to be proud of.

"It turned out nicely, didn't it? Mary Elle asked Thomas.

"Breathtaking," Thomas said, but his eyes were on Mary Elle, and as their eyes met, something shifted in the air between them. Before either of them could say anything else, the couple returned.

* * *

Now gathered around the in-house restaurant's bar, the staff celebrated the event's success.

"Mary Elle," David said, raising a glass, "congratulations on a beautiful wedding."

The rest of the team raised their glass as well.

"This wedding would not have turned out as beautifully as it did without all of you." Mary Elle said, raising her glass.

Mary Elle was delighted with how their small team had come together to make this event come to life.

She was sure that the grand reopening would be a hit as well. She felt like she could finally relax. At least until the next big event. She hoped they would receive many referrals from the guests today.

"How are you feeling?" Thomas asked, sliding onto the bar next to Mary Elle

"Relieved," Mary Elle said with a laugh.

"I probably haven't said this enough, but I am delighted you joined our team."

"As am I. I was terrified of taking this on, but I see this is exactly what I needed."

"You were made for this, Ms. Sloane."

"You think so?"

"I've seen no one handle all the hurdles thrown at you during the planning process with more grace than you."

"Piece of cake?" Lisa asked as she offered a plate to Mary Elle and Thomas.

"How could we refuse?" Mary Elle said, taking the plates from Lisa and placing them on the bar for herself and Thomas. Lisa had made the wedding cake herself from scratch, and it had been as beautiful as it was delicious. "Lisa, this is heavenly!" Mary Elle exclaimed.

Lisa was beaming, "We even had a few people approach us to say they will place orders for cakes and desserts soon."

"Wow, that is fantastic news!" Mary Elle said.

"Many people also asked about the food and said they would call in to make reservations for the restaurant," Jasper said; because of the couple's tight budget, they had opted out of having a catering company and instead had Willow Acres provide the food and refreshments. Jasper and the rest of the staff had worked as servers.

"I can imagine many people find Dean's food hard to resist," Patty said as she winked at Dean.

Dean blushed and said, "Thank you. It was exciting to have people asking for seconds."

Dean had discovered a love for food at a very young age. He had opted out of college and pursued cooking instead. Dean had applied to all the restaurants in town, but no one would give him a chance. He was a kid with minimal experience.

When Thomas heard from a friend about Dean, he

reached out to him and offered him a job as the restaurant's Sous-Chef. Once Harry retired after many decades working at Willow Acres, Dean became the head chef.

"Tonight was only the beginning. I can't wait for what the future holds for us all here." Thomas said with an almost inaudible crack in his voice, "You all have proven to me, time and time again, that you love Willow Acres just as much as I do, and I cannot thank you enough for that. I am very proud of us all. We came together today,"

"To Willow Acres!" David shouted as he led the team into a giant group hug around Thomas.

* * *

OVER THE NEXT FEW WEEKS, Willow Acres had seen a steep increase in interest from many of the town's residents. They were still trying to think of ways to bring in tourists, but the newfound attention was excellent.

Melanie had invited a food blogger friend to visit Willow Heights the following weekend. She would bring her to Willow Acres. In exchange for a review, they would provide a free meal. Dean was working on the menu that he wanted them to sample. The team was all abuzz, eager to see the attention this would bring in.

Mary Elle did not know too much about bloggers and influencers, but Melanie's excitement was contagious. It had been a very long time since she had seen Melanie this excited about anything. She loved the relationship she had with each of her kids. They wanted the best for her and wholeheartedly supported her and this new venture.

"How come no one told me?" Tiffany whined on the phone when Mary Elle told her the plan, "I want to be there too!"

Mary Elle laughed, "Honey, you're welcome to come. You know you don't need an invitation."

"Okay, pencil me in!" Tiffany said with a laugh. "I need to get away from Campus, and Willow Heights seems like just the place."

"A lot going on at school?" Mary Elle asked, concerned.

"It's the last year, so I swear they crammed every project to punish us," Tiffany said, letting out a loud groan; Mary Elle could not help but smile.

Tiffany had always been known to be just a tad bit dramatic. David appeared and took a seat in front of Mary Elle as she said her goodbyes to Tiffany.

"Is everything alright?" Mary Elle asked as she set her phone down.

"Everything is great. I just wanted you to know that Dean wants us all to stay for dinner today to sample the menu. He'll be serving the food blogger."

"I can't wait to see what he has up his sleeve."

"He won't let anyone in the kitchen, but it smells fantastic. Let's head over?" David said, standing up and looking at his watch.

"Let's go."

When they reached the restaurant, everyone was already there. Patricia was setting up the table, and Jasper brought the chairs over since they had pushed the tables together to make one seating area to enjoy dinner.

"I am starving, Dean! It smells so good. Don't keep us waiting too long." Bailey shouted so that Dean could hear her in the kitchen, "He's not letting anyone back there." She explained.

Mary Elle took a seat next to Bailey. Dean appeared with two large serving trays. As soon as he set the trays down, everyone dug in.

ABIGAIL BECK

* * *

IT WAS ALREADY DARK out by the time they finished their meal. Mary Elle stayed behind with Thomas and David to help clean up. The rest of the staff had taken off with Dean.

"Thanks for staying behind. You didn't have to do that," David said as he took a stack of dishes from Mary Elle.

"I don't mind. Being here never feels like work. Plus, it's no fun going home to an empty house."

"That is very true," Thomas said as he loaded the dishwasher.

"How have you been settling in?" David asked Mary Elle.

"I feel like this is where I've always belonged. Since I was little and used to visit with my family, I always loved the way I felt while I was here. This is home. This has always been home."

"I know what you mean. I left for college because I wanted to experience something different, but I returned as soon as I finished school. There's no place like Willow Heights."

Thomas reappeared after doing a walkthrough to make sure everything was closed up.

"Are you ready to go?" He asked Mary Elle.

"Go where?"

"I'm taking you home. It's too late for you to go alone."

"It's okay. Don't worry about me," Mary Elle said.

She knew both Thomas and David had homes on the property, and she didn't want him to go out of his way after such a long day.

"I'm not taking no for an answer," Thomas said as he held the door open for Mary Elle.

"He's stubborn. There's no use in arguing with him," David said as he dried his hands with a kitchen towel.

"Alright, let me get my things so we can go."

Thomas waited for Mary Elle next to his car, and she felt her heart make a little flip.

"What about my car?"

"You can leave it here," Thomas said with a shrug.

"How will I get to work tomorrow?"

"I'll pick you up," he said as if that was the most obvious answer.

"But..." she said before he cut her off.

"Mary Elle, it's okay. I don't mind, and it's not a bother. I'd rather know you're safe than have you drive off alone."

Mary Elle nodded and quickly got into his car. She wasn't used to this kind of chivalry, but she knew it was something she could get used to.

On the way to her house, they talked about all sorts of things, from their childhood to their favorite foods. She learned that Thomas had a sweet tooth, and chocolate was his guiltiest pleasure. Being with Thomas felt so easy.

When they reached her house, Thomas jumped out of the car and made his way to her side to open her door.

"Thank you," she said as she climbed out of his truck.

"It's my pleasure. I very much enjoy my time with you, Mary Elle," Thomas said, and, at this moment, she was glad that he couldn't see her face because she was sure she had the goofiest smile on her face.

"I very much enjoy my time with you, Thomas," Mary Elle said as she turned to face him.

Being with Thomas made her feel many things. Things she thought she would never feel again. Standing on her front porch, they were unsure of what to do next. Mary Elle thought of inviting him in, but it was too late.

"Have a good night, Mary Elle. I will be here bright and early tomorrow," Thomas said before giving Mary Elle a light kiss on the cheek.

"You too. Rest well," she finally said by the time he was already near his car.

He stopped next to his car and gave her a small wave. Mary Elle tossed and turned in bed all night, replaying that evening repeatedly with a smile on her face the whole time.

CHAPTER 13

"You're here!" Mary Elle said as she ran down her porch stairs to Melanie and Tiffany, pulling them into a tight hug.

"Mom, this is my friend Britney also known as Brit tastes the world on social media," Melanie said as she pulled away from her mother.

"It's so lovely to meet you. We are so excited to have you here." Mary Elle said as she pulled Britney into a warm embrace. She couldn't help it; she was a hugger.

"Thanks for having me. I have already seen a few spots I want to visit. I also noticed many places where I can get cool shots for my vlog," Britney said.

"Fantastic!" Mary Elle said as she helped the girls with their bags into her home.

Britney started her food blog while in college. She went to many fancy restaurants and ordered the cheapest items on the menu that she could afford on her student income and would review them. She started vlogging, and soon many of her videos went viral. What Mary Elle learned from Tiffany is an excellent thing.

ABIGAIL BECK

When a video goes viral, it becomes very popular on video-sharing websites. Mary Elle was excited to have Brittney here and see what this could do for Willow Heights and Willow Acres.

* * *

"WOW, THIS IS SUCH A SCENIC PLACE!" Brittney said as she took in the beauty all around.

"Doesn't it feel like we just stepped into a movie?" Tiffany asked.

Brittney nodded and said, "I already love it here, and I hope the food is as delicious as this place is beautiful."

They led the girls to their table. They sat on the deck by the river, which had a gorgeous view.

"Welcome to Willow Acres! I am Wyatt, and I will be your server today." The young boy said shyly, not meeting any of their eyes.

"Thanks, Wyatt! I am so excited to be here today." Brittney said, giving Wyatt her most genuine smile.

"When Dean told me you were coming, I couldn't believe it! I've been following you for a long time. I wish I could do what you do." Wyatt said, finally meeting her eyes.

"The beauty of what I do is that anyone can do it. I started with just a few followers when I lived in Kansas. I'll tell you what, start your page, and I'll be sure to give you a shout and I'll give you a follow."

"Would you really do that?" Wyatt asked with wide eyes.

"Of course, we all have to start somewhere, right?" She said with a wink.

"Thank you, Brittney. I will get right on that after work. Today we have three special meals prepared for you," Wyatt said, handing them the cocktail menus Dean had prepared for today. "Let's start with drinks. What would you all like?"

NEW BEGINNINGS IN WILLOW HEIGHTS

"I would love your Willow Acres special Iced Tea," Tiffany said as she handed the drinks menu back to Wyatt.

"I'll have the Willow Acres Lemonjito," Melanie said.

"I would like a Willowtini," Brittney chipped in.

"I'll be back with your drinks," he said as he bowed his head and took the drink menus from Melanie and Brittney.

"I think you made his day," Melanie said

Brittney shrugged her shoulders. "I remember what it's like being in a small town and looking up at all the big influencers. When I started my page, my sister and cousins were the only ones who ever gave me likes."

"Look at you now, living your dream life in New York with three million followers!" Melanie said as she took a piece of bread that the server had placed at the center of their table.

"I've come a long way from Kansas, but I never lose sight of where I started. This place has a lot to offer, and I can't wait to post all the videos and photos we've taken here."

Shortly after, Thomas appeared to welcome them and answer questions they might have about Willow Acres and its history.

"Good afternoon, ladies. I'm Thomas Clarke, and I would like to welcome you to Willow Acres."

"I've heard so much about you, Thomas; thank you for having me."

"The pleasure is all mine, Brittney."

"You have a hidden gem here," Tiffany said.

"Thank you, Tiffany. Please feel free to ask me any questions you might have about the restaurant or the farm we have here. Also, if you'd like to take a horse ride, don't be shy. We want you to see all we have to offer." Thomas said.

"That's very kind of you. We will definitely look around afterward," Brittney said

"So, Thomas, how old is Willow Acres?" Melanie asked.

89

ABIGAIL BECK

"It's been in my family for several decades. Before I took over, my father branched out from farming only. We started as a tiny diner, but as you can see, we have expanded." He said with a chuckle. "We now have the farm, where we produce many if not all the ingredients we use in our restaurant, and then we added the bakery. We also have farm animals, like the horses that we let people ride and offer riding lessons. So, the short answer is Willow Acres has been around since 1929."

"That's amazing. It's clear you, and your ancestors have put so much love into this place," Brittney said.

"Yes, I wouldn't have it any other way. My siblings and I grew up here. We tended the chickens and horses ourselves. I inherited Willow Acres from my father. Many of the employees you see are like family. They have been working here for many years. My assistant is my nephew, David. He's had a summer job here since he was 14 years old. He went to college and came back. That's how much we love this place." Thomas said with so much pride in both Willow Acres and David.

As Wyatt returned with their drinks, Thomas said, "I'll leave you girls; please enjoy your stay and let me know if there's anything you might need."

Tiffany took a sip of her Willow Acres Iced Tea. "This is the best-iced tea I've had. It's an old-fashioned tea, home-made, not that powdery stuff."

"Cheers," Brittney said, raising her glass.

"Cheers; how's your martini?" Melanie asked as they all clinked their glasses together.

"Good, dirty like I like it," Brittney said as she giggled.

"Here are your appetizers," Wyatt said, placing the plates and utensils on the table. "This one is the classic Southern spread which has deviled eggs, spiced pecans, smoked ham, pimiento cheese dip, pretzels, crackers, peach, and cherries. This one here is a bacon-wrapped jalapeño popper."

"Let's dig in," Tiffany said as she started with the Classic Southern spread.

"The fruits are fresh; I like the savory elements of this spread. I haven't tried any spread like this before," Brittney said.

"The jalapeño poppers are delicious too," Melanie said, although she had never been much into spicy food.

"Very yummy," Brittney said in between bites.

"Here are the steakhouse rib eyes with creamed spinach, and this one here is seafood gumbo," Wyatt said as he set the plates down.

"This gumbo smells so delicious," Brittney said as soon as she caught a whiff of the gumbo.

"I'll try the steakhouse rib eyes first," Tiffany added. Tiffany always went for the meatiest dish. She loved a good steak, something she had gotten from her father.

"I can taste all the flavors in my mouth. This is absolutely the best gumbo I've ever had," Brittney gushed while writing notes on her phone and taking pictures of the plates as she had been doing since they sat down.

Everything was being photographed and would be used in her blog.

"The steak is soft and not dry. I like the spinach too." Tiffany added. Soon the girls had tried both plates.

Wyatt came by to pick up the plates, clear the table, and refill drinks.

"Here are the desserts. This one is Spiked Banana Pudding, and this one is Brown Sugar Apple Crisp,"

"Both desserts were very decadent," Melanie said, whipping her lips with a napkin.

"I have only positive things to say about the services, the

location, and the food and drinks. I loved it here," Brittney said as she sat back, feeling extremely satisfied.

After eating the delicious food, the girls took a walk around Willow Acres and took a picture of the gardens, the river, the farm, the bakery, and, of course, many selfies. They also met with Jasper, who took them horse riding around the property.

* * *

Mary Elle was excited to see the girls and hear their thoughts on the meal and their experience at Willow Acres. She was speaking with Thomas when they saw the girls approaching. Thomas was also eager to hear their comments, and she could tell he had been nervous all day, though he didn't admit it.

"How was everything?" Mary Elle asked the girls as they joined her and Thomas at a picnic table.

"Everything was great! The services and meals were exquisite. Very tasteful and cozy. The décor is rustic but chic, and the river is very scenic. I enjoyed meeting with Jasper. He was very professional, yet very nice. The farm was clean, and the animals were well taken care of. The gardens are beautiful with so many kinds of flowers and plants," Brittney said as she glanced down at her notes a few times.

"This place is perfect for photoshoots," Melanie added in.

"Yes, we took amazing selfies and videos. We've been posting teasers on her social media pages all day. Everyone has been commenting on how amazing this place looks," Tiffany said, showing Mary Elle and Thomas some messages she had received from friends.

"This makes me so happy. You do not know how much this means to me," Thomas said, smiling from ear to ear.

"I am dreading having to leave tomorrow. If it weren't

because I have to attend a food and wine festival tomorrow, I would extend my stay," Brittney said with a glum look on her face.

"You're welcome to return whenever you like. You can always stay at my house. I've loved having you here," Mary Elle said, placing her hand over Brittney's.

"I'd love that, and I will come back," Brittney said with tears in her eyes, but she looked away, clearly hoping no one had noticed. Mary Elle let it go, not wanting to put Brittney on the spot, but she wondered what might be troubling her.

* * *

THE GIRLS FOUND a karaoke bar in Willow Heights that Mary Elle had never heard of. They went there for a quick bite and a fun little girl's night.

Tiffany could tell that Mary Elle was happy to be invited along with them. Though it was said that their parents had gotten divorced, Tiffany felt like this had brought her and Melanie closer to their mother.

The women each ordered a glass of sweet tea each. Mary Elle was sitting across from her, laughing at something Brittney had said. Tiffany loved that she could have this kind of relationship with her mother now as an adult.

"Those handsome guys over there sent you these," the server said, handing them a single rose.

Tiffany recognized David and Dean, her mother's coworkers, and another guy she'd never seen before.

"Hey, come join us!" Mary Elle said, waving them over. David introduced his friend, whom Tiffany hadn't recognized as his friend Cade.

They invited the guys to join them at their table, and they ordered some chips and salsa, chicken wings, and Mexican egg rolls.

"I didn't expect to see you all here," David said as the server brought a pitcher of sweet tea over.

"Tiffany likes to think she can sing and always finds karaoke bars for us to embarrass ourselves during trips," Melanie said as she dipped her chip in the salsa bowl.

"Cade likes to pretend he's a country star, so he drags us along," Dean said with a laugh.

"That explains the long hair and cowboy boots," Brittney said, eyeing Cade.

"In Cade's defense, we were all in a band together back in College," David said, slinging his arm around Cade.

As the night progressed, Tiffany noticed that David was very outgoing and hilarious. He loved making people feel comfortable and telling jokes.

Tiffany was happy to see that her mom had such carefree people around to help her at this time of her life. They weren't bad to look at either. David was a few years older than Tiffany, and he had gone to business school and was back home after graduating.

"We didn't want to interrupt you, ladies, but we didn't want to miss the chance of welcoming you to Willow Heights. We are up next. Hope you enjoy the show!" Dean said with a wink as the men made their way to the small stage at the rear of the bar.

They sang "Somebody like you" by Keith Urban and even played their own instruments. David was the vocals and guitar and serenaded Tiffany, making her blush.

Three acts later, Tiffany and the girls took the stage and went with the classic "Girls just want to have fun." The crowd joined in, and they had a great time singing and bringing back the 80s vibe.

Once they were back at the table, Mary Elle excused herself. She left the karaoke bar a little early since she had an early morning the next day to welcome Rita, who was visiting for the weekend. Rita was alone this weekend because Bob was out of town at a conference.

Mary Elle had planned some time to relax at home and catch up on things with Rita over some Mexican food. Rita had only one special request to swim in the lake and swing on the hammock.

"We're going to miss you, mom!" Melanie called out after her, and Mary Elle turned back to blow a kiss at them.

"That one was for me!" David said as he pretended to catch the kiss and pressed it to his heart.

They ordered more drinks and food and sang a few more songs. Tiffany loved seeing Melanie letting her guard down and having a good time. It had been such a long time.

"Ugh, I am never eating again," Brittney announced as she patted her full belly.

"We should probably get going. It's 4 AM." Melanie said, glancing at her watch.

"We'll drive you home," Dean said as he stood and stretched.

"Oh, don't worry about us," Melanie said as she pulled her phone out, ready to call a taxi.

"Ladies, my uncle will never forgive us if we let you go home alone," David said sternly.

"Well, if you insist..." Britney said as she stood up and looped her arm around Dean, and they made their way out.

CHAPTER 14

Mary Elle woke to the sun peeking in through her blinds. She was feeling refreshed after a great restful weekend. Rita had to cancel her plans and hadn't visited after.

Mary Elle decided the night before that today was the day that she was going to invite Thomas on the camping trip. She was nervous and unsure of what he would say. Mary Elle felt they had a connection, and she wanted to get to know him outside of work.

She hoped that being out with her family and friends wouldn't feel too much like dating and just friends getting to know each other. Friday night at the karaoke bar, she'd had a great time. She hoped that the camping trip would go just as well.

She couldn't remember the last time she'd seen her girls bonding the way they had when they went to the karaoke bar. Melanie looked in much better spirits, and she hoped that meant she'd had time to clear things with Everett.

Tiffany rarely let her guard down and only focused on her goals, which worried Mary Elle for different reasons. She knew Tiffany was limiting herself by not allowing herself to experience love. "Just because you fall in love doesn't mean you give up on your dreams and goals. It's better to have a partner in crime," she remembers telling Tiffany and Michael.

Michael was another one that worried Mary Elle. He was dating several girls, and they all seemed superficial and shallow. She wanted him to find a good woman that would love him for who he was and not for his material possessions. Finding genuine friendships and falling in love is almost impossible nowadays.

Everything was quick, and dating apps weren't always the best way to meet people, but as her kids reminded her, she was just an old-timer, so these new dating methods made little sense.

As soon as she walked into the office that morning, something felt off. When she went into the main office and clocked in, Bailey from accounting seemed highly flustered.

"Everything okay?" Mary Elle asked

"Oh, everything is fine," Bailey said, giving her a weary smile that was not very reassuring.

"Hello there, I am Mrs. Clarke. You must be the new cleaning lady?" Mary Elle turned around to see an elegantly dressed woman standing behind her.

"Hi, I'm Mary Elle. I am the events planner. Pleased to meet you," Mary Elle said as she extended her hand.

"David!" the woman exclaimed, ignoring Mary Elle completely.

"Aunt Clarice. What are you doing here?" He asked while putting his backpack away.

"Is that how you greet your auntie?"

"Sorry, I wasn't expecting you." He said while pulling her into a hug.

"I heard you all are having a grand reopening for Willow Acres. How could I miss it?"

David stood speechless with a confused smile on his face. Mary Elle did not know who this woman was, but she was sure she was the reason for Bailey's odd behavior earlier.

"Now, where's my husband?" Clarice asked.

"Uncle Thomas must be out by the cabins," David said as he tried to steer Clarice away and shot Mary Elle an apologetic smile.

"When I heard y'all hired an event planner, I thought you would've hired someone young and hip. Not an old lady." Clarice said, just high enough for Mary Elle to hear.

Mary Elle didn't mind that low jab; she was still trying to understand how this woman was Thomas' wife. How had she not known he was married? Had she made everything up in her head? She thought they had a connection.

* * *

"OH, COME ON!" Mary Elle muttered in frustration while untangling the white lights she'd found in storage. She avoided Thomas and tried to do anything possible to stay out of the office today.

She felt like a fool and was so embarrassed that she'd almost asked a married man on a camping trip. What had she been thinking? It took all of her self-control to stop herself from grabbing the lights and tossing them out of view.

Every time she untangled them, they instantly got tangled again. She thought it would be good to put the lights on the trees near the cabins, but she questioned that idea altogether now. After about 30 minutes of untangling the lights, she grabbed a small ladder and adorned the trees.

She had been so lost in thought that she hadn't noticed how far up the tree she had climbed. While trying to climb down, she missed a step, and before she knew it, tumbling down, she went.

The pain was so bad she feared she was going to pass out. She tries to get up, but the pain is too much. She frantically starts calling for help.

"Help! Help!" She feels panic creep in when she worries no one will hear her.

"Someone, please help!" She tries to pull herself up, but the pain is too much. She wishes she'd thought to bring her cellphone, but it's tucked away in her purse back at the office.

"Help!" she calls out again.

"Mary Elle! Are you okay? What happened?" Thomas appears and crouches next to her.

"I fell from the tree while trying to hang the lights. I can't get up," she says as she tries again and fails.

"Where does it hurt?" he asks as he studies her, unsure of what to do.

"Everything hurts."

Mary Elle expected Thomas to yell at her and make her feel bad for even thinking about climbing the tree. In hindsight, she knows it wasn't her best idea. She just couldn't help herself. Once she got a vision going, she wanted to see it come to fruition as soon as possible.

Thomas slowly and carefully checks on her legs. "Does this hurt?" He asks as he slowly moves her ankle around. Thomas seems so far away now that Mary Elle can barely hear him.

"Stay awake. I'm going to get some help." That's the last thing Mary Elle hears him say when suddenly everything goes dark.

* * *

ABIGAIL BECK

WHEN SHE FINALLY COMES, she's greeted by very bright lights and a faint beeping sound. What happened? Where am I? She thinks as she blinks to adjust her eyes and sit up.

"Mary Elle, thank God you're awake!" Thomas says as he appears next to her. His face is full of emotions, and she can hear the relief in his voice.

"What happened?"

"Doctor says you have a sprained ankle and might have a concussion. You're also going to have a lot of bruising, but you'll be okay." Thomas says as he strokes her hand.

Mary Elle tries to adjust herself on the bed and winces in pain.

"Does my family know I'm here?"

"I found your sister's number on your phone and called her. She said she'd let your kids know."

"My sister?"

"Hi there, big sis." Mary Elle hears someone say, and even though it's been years, she recognizes the voice instantly.

DeeAnn comes into view, holding two coffee cups, and hands one to Thomas. She looks exactly like the social media posts Mary Elle often saw online.

She was about a foot taller than Mary Elle and had big bouncy curls. They looked nothing alike but shared the same blue eyes their mother had passed down to them.

"DeeAnn... I can't believe you're here," Mary Elle says and feels tears forming in her eyes.

"I came as soon as I heard. You scared me to death! I was afraid I'd be too late," DeeAnn says and clears her throat.

"I'm sorry..."

"No, I'm sorry," DeeAnn says, now standing at Mary Elle's bedside and taking her other hand in hers.

Mary Elle suddenly realizes that Thomas is holding her other hand and feels a blush come on. Her sister must have many questions but doesn't seem to give them away.

NEW BEGINNINGS IN WILLOW HEIGHTS

"I'm going to head out to the farm. Call me if you need anything. I'm sure everyone will be happy to hear that you're okay," Thomas says, giving Mary Elle's hand one last squeeze.

* * *

MARY ELLE HAS BEEN ENJOYING the last few days with her sister. It wasn't under the circumstances that she would've liked, but her sister was here, and she would not let their time go to waste.

DeeAnn had refused to leave Mary Elle's side and insisted on staying in the recliner next to Mary Elle. Thomas had been great as well. Every morning he would bring breakfast for her and DeeAnn. Mary Elle had always been the caretaker for everyone, and she wasn't used to this kind of treatment. Especially not from a man.

He constantly asked her how she was feeling and if there was anything she needed. Thomas was such a great man, and here he was, taking care of her. He barely knew her, but he was by her side, ensuring she was okay. Bill never would've done that. He would've seen that she was okay and rushed back to his office, never giving her a second thought.

She had to keep reminding herself that Thomas was a married man, and he was simply a gentleman. Every time she remembered, she felt a slight pang in her chest. She wasn't upset at him anymore, though - it wasn't his fault that she'd misconstrued his kindness for anything more.

"Mary Elle, you're being discharged today. The observation period is over, and the doctor gave orders to discharge you," Donna, her lovely nurse, said.

"Thank you for all your help while I was here," Mary Elle said as Donna made notes on her chart.

"It's been a pleasure having you stay with us. I can't wait to go visit Willow Acres," Donna said.

ABIGAIL BECK

"Ask for me when you go by. We'll make it worth your while," Thomas said to her.

"Will do," Donna said as she continued the discharge process with Mary Elle.

"I'll go get the car," Thomas announced and quickly headed out of the room.

"You got fortunate with him," Donna said, giving Mary Elle a light nudge.

Mary Elle didn't correct her and tell her that it was her boss, even though she knew she should. She couldn't help that a small part of her liked that Donna thought she and Thomas were a couple.

* * *

MARY ELLE SAT AWKWARDLY in the wheelchair the doctor insisted she go down in. DeeAnn sat next to her as they waited for Thomas to pull up.

She felt the urge to ask DeeAnn to stay with her for a few days. She was nervous, but she knew it was now or never.

"Hey Dee, would you be able to stay with me for a few days?" Mary Elle asked as she braced herself for her sister's response.

"I would love to. I packed a small bag in case things were bad here," DeeAnn said, giving Mary Elle's shoulder a light squeeze.

"I am so glad you came. It means so much to me. We have a lot to catch up on,"

"We sure do! How in the world did you end up here? Where is Bill? I have so many questions."

"We will probably need a few drinks before we dive into that," Mary Elle replied with a giggle.

"I'm dying to know who this handsome Thomas taking care of you is? He said he was your boss?"

"Yes, I started working for him when I moved here. It's kind of my dream job, to be honest. I'm enjoying the simpler, quieter life out here."

"Wow, never in a million years would I have thought that you'd move out of the city without Bill. However, I have very fond memories of being here with you, mom, and dad. I miss those days. I miss them."

Some tears were filling up Mary Elle's eyes, just remembering how her dad taught them to ride a bike by the lake and how her mom would bake them pies during their time spent here.

"I sure miss them too," Mary Elle replied.

Thomas dropped them off, and once he made sure they had everything they needed, he headed out. His wife was one lucky lady, Mary Elle thought.

As soon as they got home, DeeAnn ran right up to her old room, the same as when they were kids. Their parents had never remodeled or moved any of the furniture around.

Mary Elle went down to the basement to get the boxes with the old photos. She couldn't wait to show her all the photos she had found taken of them during all those summers and even Christmas vacations.

"Look what I got," Mary Elle said, putting the boxes down next to the coffee table.

"I can't believe we have so many photo albums," DeeAnn said as she started going through them.

"Oh, my goodness, look at your haircut in this photo!" Mary Elle said, pointing at the photos with DeeAnn's homemade haircut.

Their mom had been so proud of the outcome of DeeAnn's haircut after she got gum stuck on it. It wasn't the best haircut because their mother was no hairstylist and had left the hair so short that DeeAnn didn't want the other kids

ABIGAIL BECK

at camp to see it. It took a long time for her hair to grow out again.

"Aw, look, this is a baby photo of you, Mary Elle. You were such a chubby baby. Look at those cheeks."

"Can you believe they took so many photos of us? I never knew until I found the boxes."

"Crazy, isn't it? Look, there's you and dad when he was teaching you how to ride the bike," DeeAnn said as she leaned over to give Mary Elle a better glimpse.

"He was the man that loved me the most. I miss him so much." Mary Elle said with a sigh.

"So, what happened with Bill?" DeeAnn asked again.

"Well, he had an affair, and you'll never guess with who."

"With Rita?"

"Oh no. Could you imagine? With Barbara. You remember her, don't you?"

"With her? No way!"

"Yeah, I still can't believe it. Having an affair was bad, but it was with her was just the biggest slap in the face."

"I can't imagine. Is that how you ended up here?"

"I couldn't stand being in that house anymore. Everything reminded me of him. I hated going out too because everyone knew. Barbara made it a point to let everyone know. I was so embarrassed. I did not know what was going on. So, I jumped into my car, and somehow the road led me here. I decided this was what I needed. A quieter, slower lifestyle."

"Wow, I'm so sorry that you had to deal with all that."

"It's okay. I'm here now, and I wholeheartedly believe this is where I am supposed to be."

"One of my greatest regrets has been not being around for you. I'm sorry about that." DeeAnn said as her voice cracked

"Oh, Dee. It's okay." Mary Elle said, placing a hand on her sister's knee.

"It's not. I blamed you for so long for things that had nothing to do with you, and I'm sorry."

"It's ok, DeeAnn. We were young and dumb. We all did things we regret." Though Mary Elle never knew what had caused the rift in their relationship, she didn't want to waste any time now. It did no one any good to dig up old wounds.

"I am starving. Should we make something to eat?"

"Why don't we go out to dinner? There are many great restaurants on the square that I haven't yet visited."

"Sounds good. Let's freshen up and head out in about 30 minutes?"

SITTING across the table from DeeAnn, Mary Elle couldn't believe how much her life had changed. She loved having her sister around; she had lost hope of ever having a relationship with her long ago. Mary Elle had missed her sister so much. Although she knew that eventually, they would have to discuss whatever had torn them apart, she chose to focus on the present moment for now.

"Should we get dessert?" DeeAnn asked while leafing through the dessert menu. One thing that had always united them while growing up was their love for sweets. They would often sneak into the kitchen once their parents went to bed to gorge on the ice cream.

"How could we not?" Mary Elle said with a laugh

They ordered a decadent brownie with vanilla ice cream and cherries on top.

"Mmm," they said in unison as the brownie made their taste buds explode in satisfaction. Their eyes locked, and they broke into a fit of giggles.

Mary Elle felt a shift in the atmosphere, and DeeAnn's face went sour out of nowhere.

"What's wrong?" Mary Elle asked while trying to see what had upset her sister.

"Oh, nothing. I thought I'd seen someone, but I was wrong." She said, smiling wearily, but Mary Elle could tell she was lying.

"Mary Elle, is that you?" said a familiar voice, and Mary Elle's back instantly straightened.

DeeAnn shot her an apologetic look.

"Clarice... Hi! This is my sister, DeeAnn. Dee, this is Thomas's wife."

"Pleased to meet you," DeeAnn said, though her tone said otherwise.

"I heard about your little tumble. Glad to see you are doing better. Would probably be for the best to tell one of the young people to do that sort of thing next time?"

DeeAnn cleared her throat, and before she released any spitfire on Clarice, Mary Elle gave her a warning look and said, "Of course. I learned my lesson," with a tight smile.

"Thomas is waiting for me at the bar. We ordered pick up. See you around, ladies."

"Thomas is married?" DeeAnn asked as soon as Clarice was out of earshot.

"Yeah." Mary Elle said, dropping her head

"I thought...."

"Yeah. Me too. I almost made the mistake of asking him out!" Mary Elle said with a sad laugh, which resulted in DeeAnn bursting into laughter.

"I'm sorry. I know it is not funny. I just cannot believe our luck in men. Mom would be beside herself."

"Have you also been having a hard time dating?"

"Oh, you have no idea. I thought it would get better as we got older, but no. Men don't get any better as they age."

"I guess we'll have to keep looking, but you know what they say? That love comes when you least expect it,"

"Very true. Anyway, what other plans do you have for this summer?" DeeAnn said, changing the subject

"Nothing special. My romantic summer ideas are now nonexistent," Mary Elle replied

"I'm sure you'll have a great summer. I want this year to be different. We haven't spent any holidays together as a family for a long time. Would you mind arranging with the kids to see if they're up for it?"

"I'm sure they would love that. We usually spend the holidays together, but I'm not sure how things will go with the Bill situation now. Anyway, I'll ask them and let you know soon,"

CHAPTER 15

DeeAnn was enjoying her time in Willow Heights; Being in Willow Heights felt like home. Here, she had spent all her summers and where she had created some of her favorite memories.

She had her first kiss here and her first boyfriend. She learned how to ride a bike, and her mother taught her how to make shepherd's pie. When their family came to Willow Heights was when they could let go of everything else.

Her dad wasn't a businessman when he was here. He was just their dad. Their mother wasn't a busy housewife. In Willow Heights, they came together, and they could be a family.

She hoped she could recreate that now with Mary Elle. She wanted to fix things, and she didn't want to be estranged from her family anymore.

DeeAnn had spent most of her adult life working as a middle school teacher. She enjoyed working with young, curious minds, but the best part of the job was having summers off. She had dedicated her summers to going on cross-country trips and traveling worldwide.

DeeAnn never had a real adult relationship and did most of her traveling alone - meeting loads of interesting people. The problem was that once she wasn't galloping around the world, she returned to her home, where she was all alone.

There was something about the quiet, slow pace of life of Willow Heights that made her feel at peace. She almost felt like maybe she deserved a second chance.

She especially enjoyed the time she was getting to spend with her sister. After her parents passed away, she realized how foolish she'd been all these years and that she should repair her relationship with Mary Elle. She hadn't acted on it because she didn't know where to start. DeeAnn didn't know if Mary Elle wanted anything to do with her and, if we're being honest, she was too much of a coward to make the first move.

AS SHE WALKED along the lake, she thought about everything she would love to do with Mary Elle. But there was still something nagging at her. In the back of her mind, she knew she had to come clean to her sister. She owed her an explanation for pushing her away.

Mary Elle had been nothing but kind towards her, no matter how often she'd lashed out. She could blame it on being a dumb teenager, but she'd known she was in the wrong even as a young adult. Would their relationship ever be the same? Could Mary Elle ever truly forgive her?

She felt a tear slide down her face. She had worked on herself and had forgiven her parents before they passed away, but her sister had been her very best friend, and it broke her heart thinking back on how badly she'd mistreated her.

"Hi there," Mrs. Adelman said as she pruned her roses in her backyard.

"I didn't see you there," DeeAnn said as she walked over to the older woman. Mrs. Adelman wore an adorable polka dot dress with her trusty orthopedic fisherman sandals. She had always been a fashionista, and DeeAnn had always admired that about her. When DeeAnn had her first date one summer, she had sneakily given her a bright red lipstick to wear.

"You seemed lost in thought. Is everything okay?"

"Things are okay. Mind if I join you?"

"Feel free." Mrs. Adelman said as she waved her over, and her gold bangles clashed together. "I'll go get us a pitcher of sweet tea. I'll be right back."

She returned a few minutes later with a pitcher of sweet tea and a couple of juniper green drinking glasses.

"I'm so happy to see you, girls, back here," She said as she placed the items on the patio table.

"I honestly never thought I would ever come back here. Now that I'm here, I don't think I want to leave," DeeAnn said with a sad laugh as she took a seat across from Mrs. Adelman.

"Why do you have to leave?"

"I have no place to stay, and I have a job back home."

"I'm sure your sister would love for you to stay with her, and I don't know if you know this, but we have schools here too."

"My sister and I haven't had the best relationship."

"Oh, I know. I remember how close you used to be as young girls playing out here. I also remember how it broke your mother's heart when you had a falling out."

"I was a very dumb kid."

"We all did dumb things growing up. You have a chance now to mend that relationship. Don't waste another day - many people don't get a second chance."

As they finished plucking out the weeds and pruning the roses, DeeAnn thought about what Mrs. Adelman said.

She knew she was right. She had a second chance, and she shouldn't let it go to waste. DeeAnn just hoped that Mary Elle could forgive her someday. Will they be able to go back to the way things were before? Was she fooling herself?

* * *

DINNER WAS A HOME-COOKED MEAL. It was a chicken pot pie. The ladies loved this, as it reminded them of their parents.

DeeAnn thought about expressing her thoughts to Mary Elle during dinner, but she never found the nerve to do it. They had peach cobbler for dessert. The peach cobbler had been their mother's specialty, and she insisted they learn how to make it at a young age. It was a family favorite, and they enjoyed it many nights during their summers spent here.

Mary Elle had also served a dollop of vanilla ice cream to accompany it. Willow heights still made ice cream the old-fashioned way, and they sold it in their little local shop.

"Mary Elle, I've been thinking..." DeeAnn said, hesitant and nervous that she might say the wrong thing.

She didn't want to ruin their relationship further if she said something without thinking it through.

"Yes, Dee? What is it?"

"I just wanted to say that it's been so incredible to be here with you these past few days. I've been thinking about our childhood, and this house brings back so many memories."

"I've loved having you here and reconnecting with you." Mary Elle said.

"I'm sorry about what's happened between us. It's a late apology, and we've grown up estranged because of me, but I love you, and you're all I have left. I want to fix our relationship."

ABIGAIL BECK

"DeeAnn, of course, I forgive you, and just like you - I want to fix things with you and reconnect. I was planning on asking you to stay because I saw you so much happier here. You've got this calm about you when you're here. I know it's a lot to ask because you have a life in Savannah, but I would love to have you here with me."

"Then it's settled. I am moving to Willow Heights as soon as I'm done with summer school!" DeeAnn said and gave Mary Elle the biggest hug she'd ever given her.

* * *

"DEEANN, LOOK WHAT I FOUND," Mary Elle said as she came down the stairs. She'd spent all morning sorting through things in the attic.

DeeAnn had been having a lazy day lounging on the sofa with Mittens, a tiny kitten she had found in their backyard a couple of days before.

Mittens was white, with little gray paws that looked like she was wearing mittens.

"What is it?" DeeAnn asked as she sat up.

"It's all kinds of letters and photographs from Grandma Helen sent to dad."

"Oh," DeeAnn quickly realized how her disappointment sounded and hoped that Mary Elle hadn't noticed.

"What's wrong?" Mary Elle asked, not missing a beat.

DeeAnn sighed. Eventually, she knew this would come up, but she didn't know where to start. "Mary Elle... there's something you don't know."

"What is it?" Mary Elle said, taking a seat, a look of concern all over her face.

"Mom had an affair on dad, and grandma Helen found out. She tried to get dad to leave mom, but they stayed together."

"Mom had an affair?"

"That's not all..." DeeAnn said as all the memories came flooding back to her. All the pain and feelings of betrayal plagued her at a young age. "Mom got pregnant from the affair. I'm the product of that affair."

Mary Elle stared at DeeAnn at a loss for words.

"That is why I changed towards you. Because every time I looked at you, I realized just how different we were. Mom and dad always said it was because I took after her side of the family, and you took after dad, but that wasn't true."

"How did you find out?"

"I found a letter from Grandma Helen. She told him he was making a mistake staying with mom and raising another man's child."

"Why didn't you tell me?"

"I was angry and hurt. I thought that if you found out, you would treat me differently. Honestly, I thought you wouldn't see me as your sister anymore. So, I pushed you away before you had a chance to."

Mary Elle pulled DeeAnn into a hug. There was something about hugging Mary Elle that made DeeAnn feel lighter. After all these years of carrying this secret by herself, it was good to let it out. She felt hopeful.

At that moment, she knew things would never be the same. DeeAnn knew she wasn't alone in the world anymore. She had her sister again. She had a family, and she had a place where she belonged.

"You're my sister. My one and only sister. Nothing will ever change that." Mary Elle said as she hugged DeeAnn tighter.

* * *

ABIGAIL BECK

DeeAnn and Mary Elle sat on the back deck on Adirondack chairs overlooking the lake and mountains. They came here every night to wind down with some warm tea.

Things between them felt different now that Mary Elle knew the truth. They'd stayed up all night talking things out, and DeeAnn felt a great sense of relief. She felt like things might go back to normal for them.

"You belong here, Mary Elle. The mountain life suits you." DeeAnn said as she watched Mary Elle sitting on the Adirondack chair, looking up at the sky. You could see an array of stars that the city lights would dim in Atlanta.

"Do you think so?" Mary Elle asked, looking over at her.

"Are you kidding? Mom and dad bought this house because of you."

"I can't imagine being here without you. I am so glad I fell off that tree," Mary Elle said.

The first time they had visited Willow Heights, the girls had fallen in love with the mountains. Willow Heights had stolen their heart from a very young age. Mary Elle would tell everyone that she'd buy a house here and raise a family when she grew up.

Bill was never a small-town kind of guy. He had big dreams and ambitions that would seem impossible to accomplish in Willow Heights. Once Mary Elle fell head over heels for Bill, she took on his dreams and goals and made them her priority. She left behind all her childhood dreams and worked on his.

"Hey, did anyone order some wine?" Rita asked as she appeared with a bottle of wine and a reusable bag full of snacks.

"Rita! I didn't know you were coming," Mary Elle said as she jumped out of her seat and made her way to her dear friend.

DeeAnn stood back and watched as the two best friends embraced, and she felt a slight twinge in her gut. The three of them had been very close once upon a time. Even though it had been DeeAnn to push them away, she had always been a bit envious of Mary Elle and Rita's relationship.

"I wanted to surprise you two. I knocked, but no one answered. Your car was out front, so I knew you were home. This place is beautiful." Rita said as she looked around.

"Rita... it's been so long." DeeAnn said as she made her way over, feeling very unsure of herself. She wasn't sure what Rita knew or how she would react to seeing her here.

Rita put the things down and enveloped DeeAnn in a big bear hug. "It's so good to see you! I could hardly believe it when Mary Elle said you were here. I'd have been here sooner, but my husband Robert hasn't felt his best."

"I hope he's okay."

"I sure hope so, too. They're doing some tests, so we'll know what's going on soon. Enough about Bob," Rita said, waving her hand, "Tell me about you; how have you been?"

The ladies sat on the Adirondack chairs while sipping wine and enjoying the spinach dip Rita had brought over. They played catch up, and it felt like they had never been apart. DeeAnn felt like she fit right in and forever wanted to remember this feeling.

CHAPTER 16

Mary Elle sat across from James for a quick lunch date at The Grit on the square. She ordered her favorite apple pecan chicken salad with a raspberry vinaigrette and James ordered a club sandwich with fries.

James owned a small antique shop on Main Street. They first met when Mary Elle purchased a few pieces from his store for her home. They had also bumped into each other a few times out and about town. James was a very easy-going man, and conversation between them was easy.

It had surprised Mary Elle when James asked her out for lunch a couple of days ago. She had been grabbing a cup of coffee with DeeAnn at the local bakery before work.

Her first thought was to turn him down nicely, but DeeAnn stood nearby and smiled encouragingly at her, so she went along with it. She was a single woman, and saying yes to new experiences was her new thing.

"So, how are you enjoying living in Willow Heights?" James asked

"I'm feeling like a local. It's great being back here."

"I, for one, am thrilled that you are here," James said as his cellphone rang. He excused himself and stepped aside to take the call.

It was then that Mary Elle noticed Thomas and Clarice sitting on the other side of the room. Thomas and Mary Elle's eyes locked, and he had a look on his face that she couldn't quite place. Was it disappointment?

"I'm sorry, that was the shop, and I had to take it. So where were we?" James said as he slid back into his seat.

Mary Elle and James had a pleasant lunch. She enjoyed his company, but she could not stop thinking about Thomas. She knew it was wrong, but she couldn't help herself.

Mary Elle had felt a connection with him. She had caught herself constantly glancing over at Thomas and Clarice, and many times, she had seen Thomas watching her. Was it all in her head? Thankfully, Clarice had been sitting with her back to her and had not noticed that she was there.

Mary Elle was now waiting for James outside the restaurant while checking work emails on her phone. The restaurant's owner had asked James to check an antique desk he had in his office to provide him with a quote.

"Was that a date you were on with James?" Thomas asked Mary Elle as he stepped out of the restaurant.

"Hello there, Thomas. Yes, I was. We had a great lunch. He's a delightful man."

"I didn't realize you were dating so soon after your divorce."

"Well, Thomas, my marriage was over long before we separated. I never thought you would judge me for dating," Mary Elle said, defending herself, something she hadn't done in a long time. Usually, she kept quiet in hopes of not causing drama. But this new Mary Elle wasn't afraid to speak up for herself.

"Oh, I'm not judging you. I am sorry if it is coming out

that way. It's just that if I would've known...." he said, letting his sentence trail off.

"If you would've known?"

"Nothing. Never mind."

"Oh, hey there!" Clarice said, looping her arm around his.

"Hi, Clarice. Lovely top." Mary Elle said sarcastically.

Clarice was wearing a bright red low-cut top that was very snug and showed off her cleavage. She also wore skintight jeans and thigh-high leather boots with a stiletto heels. Mary Elle did not know how someone like Thomas could be with Clarice.

"Thanks, Mary Elle. We should go shopping together sometime. It might be time for a refresh on your wardrobe."

"Clarice, we should get going. Don't you have a doctor's appointment?" Thomas asks, clearly feeling uncomfortable as he tries to slip his arm away from Clarice.

"That's right. Lead the way, Thomas," Clarice said as she dragged Thomas away.

Thomas turned around and said, "I'll see you back at the office, Mary Elle."

Mary Elle watched as they walked over to his car and how he opened the door for her. It hadn't been long since he had done that for her. That chicken salad was no longer sitting well in her stomach.

* * *

MARY ELLE WAS HAVING a lazy weekend. She was feeling down, and she didn't feel like doing anything. Instead, she lounged on her sofa, watching an infomercial about a vacuum cleaner that was also a mop. She was about to call in and place an order when her doorbell went off.

The night before, her previous neighbor Charlotte called

to tell her that Bill and Barbara had just purchased a new house together.

Mary Elle knew it should not bother her, but she couldn't help feeling hurt. It had been such a long time since she had let herself feel down over Bill, but today she felt like she was drowning. She wasn't sure what was making her feel this way. Perhaps it was the fact that she'd gotten her hopes up about Thomas, only to be let down all over again.

"Coming!" she called out while she slipped into her house slippers and headed towards the door.

When she opened the door, she found Mrs. Adelman standing there.

"Hey there, pretty lady," Mrs. Adelman said while handing Mary Elle a warm Pyrex that smelled delicious and made Mary Elle's stomach instantly grumble. She'd been so busy feeling sorry for herself that she hadn't had anything to eat all day.

"Mrs. Adelman, it's so good to see you. Please come in." Mary Elle said, holding the door open for her.

"The place looks great. Your parents would've loved the little touches you'd added to it," Mrs. Adelman said as she took in the house. "It's looking like your home now."

"Thank you, and I can never thank you enough for watching after the house all these years," Mary Elle said as they walked into the kitchen.

"Mary Elle..." Mrs. Adelman said, and Mary Elle instantly noticed the uncertainty in her voice.

"Yes, Mrs. Adelman? Is everything alright?"

"You know I've never been one to beat around the bush, so I'm just going to come out and say it. What's this I hear of you going on a date with James? What about Thomas?"

"Thomas? He's married."

"Married?" Mrs. Adelman exclaimed with a laugh. "That man hasn't been married in over a decade!"

ABIGAIL BECK

"What are you saying? What about Clarice?"

"Clarice? That vile woman will try anything to get back into his life. Honey, that man has it in for you, and men like that don't come around often." She said with a tsk and a raised brow.

Mary Elle couldn't believe what she was hearing. Could it be true? Could there possibly be a chance for her and Thomas to be together? Now she felt like a childish fool pushing him away instead of talking things out like an adult.

"But when she showed up at Willow Acres, she introduced herself as his wife."

"Of course she did." Mrs. Adelman said with an eye roll, "That woman is so ridiculous."

"I have been wondering how someone like Thomas could be with someone like Clarice."

"She wasn't always like this. She moved here right after her first husband passed away. Clarice worked at the Busy Bee Coffee Shop, and that is how she and Thomas met. Clarice was very soft-spoken and timid back then. The Clarice we know now is nothing like the woman she was before." Mrs. Adelman said as she took a seat, and Mary Elle joined her.

"Thomas was never a ladies' man. He always kept to himself, and he spent all his free time at Willow Acres. Clarice weaseled herself into his life, and they got married. Thomas had always watched after his mother, and Clarice would not accept it. She wanted him to get rid of her by putting her in a nursing home, but he always refused."

"Did she say that?" Mary Elle asked in disbelief

"Oh yes, she had no shame. Margaret, his mother, was a little firecracker, and she stood up to her, which, of course, did not make things any easier for Thomas. Poor Thomas was constantly in the middle of the two women's disagreements."

"I can't imagine that living situation being easy for anyone."

"He took care of his late mother until she passed. Clarice hated not having his undivided attention. Their marriage only lasted a couple of years. Clarice eventually left him one day without a warning because she had met someone else. She always tries to weasel herself back into his life, but he doesn't budge. He's moved on, and she has never accepted his decision and, in her denial, she kept his last name after they divorced and makes an appearance now and then when her life is in shambles, hoping he will rescue her."

"What does she need rescuing from this time?"

"Who knows? Thomas is an honorable man and will always help anyone in need, even if it is Clarice."

"He's a great man. I'm sure she's realized that now, and that's why she won't let him go."

"Thomas is one of a kind. We're all rooting for you two."

"Who is we?"

"Oh, just us ladies from the club. We've been taking bets on how long it would take you two to get together." Mrs. Adelman said as a blush crept up her cheeks. The club was the bingo club that she was the President of, and they met every Tuesday and Thursday at Willow Acres.

Mary Elle could not believe they had been taking bets on her love life, and she could not help but laugh.

"Well, I hope you enjoy the casserole I made you. It was your mother's favorite." Mrs. Adelman said as she made her way to the door.

"Thank you, I can't wait to try it," Mary Elle said as she pulled Mrs. Adelman into a deep embrace.

Mary Elle closed the door behind Mrs. Adelman and did a happy dance. Thomas was single, and she was ready to mingle. She couldn't wait to tell DeeAnn. Her day was looking a lot better.

CHAPTER 17

The crew was hosting the Grand Reopening of Willow Heights. There was a lot riding on this event and they wanted to make it extra special. The sun was shining, and the flowers were all in full bloom. It was the most beautiful spring day.

Mary Elle was in a great mood after learning from Mrs. Adelman that Thomas and Clarice weren't together. She had tried to speak to Thomas privately, but Clarice had not left his side all day.

"Wow, that looks really nice!" Patty said as she stopped in her tracks on the way to the garden

"Thanks! I got an idea from a magazine and I wasn't sure if I could recreate it." As she stood back and admired the balloon arch she had worked on all morning, Mary Elle said.

"Are you sure you weren't an artist in your past life?" Patty said,

Mary Elle laughed, "Patty, you are much too kind." She had made the balloon arch of all different sizes of balloons in sage, white, and gold.

Mary Elle left the balloon arch in the storage barn for

safekeeping. Their budget was tight, and balloons were a much more affordable option than flowers. Once she was sure that the balloon arch was out of harm's way, she moved on to work on the centerpieces.

The day before, she had found lanterns in storage and spray painted them in gold. She would add baby's breath and green foliage to adorn the base using flowers they had hand-picked from the garden. She and Patty worked quietly side by side, preparing the centerpieces.

Mary Elle and Patty hadn't been working for long when they heard a loud crash. They looked at each other and ran out to see what had happened. They found a small gathering outside the storage barn, and Mary Elle's heart dropped. She knew before she saw it that the balloon arch was destroyed.

"What happened?" She asked as she approached the group.

"The brakes didn't work, and I crashed into your arch. I am so sorry, Mary Elle. I know how hard you worked on this all morning." Clarice said as she sat on the ground with Thomas crouched down next to her.

Mary Elle made her way inside the barn to access the damage. She couldn't believe her eyes when she saw that the golf cart had destroyed the balloon arch.

David had been studying the balloon arch and looked at Mary Elle with pity before saying, "I'm sorry."

"It's okay," she said with a tight smile. She wanted to believe that it was an accident and that Clarice wouldn't purposely destroy the arch, but a part of her knew better.

"I think we can salvage it," David said.

"How?"

"Come, let's get to work."

They couldn't fix the plastic frame for the balloon arch that Mary Elle had ordered online. Thankfully, David welded something together to use as the frame.

ABIGAIL BECK

While they had been working on the frame, Thomas had purchased more balloons. With Patty's help, they could blow up all the balloons necessary with a helium machine they had rented and assembled the arch. It was crunch time, and they still had a lot to go.

Bailey from accounting had also volunteered to get everything together. Dean and Jasper had set up the tables in the barn. The entire team had come together, and Mary Elle's vision for the event was coming alive.

"I'm sorry about what happened," Bailey said to Mary Elle as they finished up the centerpieces.

"It's okay - accidents happen."

"That's the thing... I don't think it was an accident."

"Why?" Mary Elle asked, stopping what she was doing and facing Bailey.

Bailey looked around to make sure no one was around before continuing and, in a hushed tone, said, "Clarice feels threatened by you, and we all know she's not the nicest person."

"Threatened? But I would never do anything to her."

"Clarice has remarried three times already since she and Thomas divorced. She always comes back around after each breakup. This time she didn't expect to find you here."

"Thomas is just my boss. Nothing is going on between us."

"Thomas is a wonderful man, and he deserves a second chance at love. We all see the way he looks at you, Mary Elle. Don't tell me you haven't noticed?"

"I thought he was being nice. I wasn't sure if I imagined things."

"You weren't imagining things, and you'd be a fool not to give him a chance."

"I wanted to ask him to join me for a camping trip with

my family so that I could get to know him out of work, but I backed out when I met Clarice."

"You should still ask him!"

"I don't know..."

"What if we gather some more of the team for the trip, so there's less pressure? Thomas loves getting everyone together."

"That sounds like a better idea." That idea had popped into her mind before, but having Bailey invite him instead of her made her feel so much better.

Maybe she was a chicken, but she didn't know how to handle rejection.

"Okay then, it's a deal! I'll invite the others and Thomas. Could you leave it to me? Just tell me the dates you were thinking of, and I'll handle it."

Mary Elle was glad to have a friend like Bailey in Willow Heights. She knew Bailey was right, Thomas was a fantastic man, and she would love to see a future with him.

Why should she let someone like Clarice get in the middle of them? Especially after what Mrs. Adelman said. Shouldn't he approach her about it? But if he had feelings for her, the way everyone kept telling her—why hadn't he made a move? Had things changed for him now that Clarice was back?

THE REST of the night took off with no other hiccups. The guests loved the food and the decor. David had also prepared a presentation showcasing all the other services offered, like horseback riding lessons, petting zoo, the summer and winter camps for the kids, and new programs that he was working on launching.

Mary Elle had lost count of how many times people had

ABIGAIL BECK

come over to compliment her work. She should have enjoyed the night, but she kept replaying Bailey's comments. As she and the rest of the crew cleaned up the barn, she couldn't stop thinking about it.

She was furious at Clarice. How could she be so childish to destroy her work out of jealousy? This wasn't high school. They were adults, and they should be able to communicate.

As if she had summoned her with her thoughts, Clarice walked into the barn, and Mary Elle let out a small groan.

"Patty, you left some trash bags behind," Clarice said as she arched an eyebrow and pointed at some bags.

"Maybe you should help her?" Mary Elle said, not able to hold her tongue any longer.

Clarice pretended she didn't hear Mary Elle and said, "Is something wrong with your arm, Patricia? Can you only carry bags with one hand?"

Overhearing the conversation, Dean went for the other trash bags and helped Patty out.

"What is wrong with you?" Mary Elle asked, now stepping in front of Clarice.

"Do not speak to me like that."

"Everyone is doing a great job working together, and you always have to step in and ruin the atmosphere."

Clarice's face went red, and she grabbed a handful of the left-over cake on a table nearby and threw it at Mary Elle.

"What are you doing?" Mary Elle said as she angrily wiped the cake off her face and clothes.

Clarice said nothing and grabbed more cake and flung it at Mary Elle.

Before she realized what she was doing, Mary Elle grabbed a handful of cake and smeared it all over the front of Clarice's dress, and smiled smugly.

"Oh, my god! You've ruined it!" Clarice exclaimed as she looked down at the damage.

NEW BEGINNINGS IN WILLOW HEIGHTS

Mary Elle quickly grabbed some more handfuls of cake and flung them at Clarice while she tried to gain a distance away from her.

Clarice grabbed a punch bowl and ran after Mary Elle. Just as she was about to dump the punch on Mary Elle, the barn door opened, and she splashed the punch all over David.

* * *

NOW SITTING IN THOMAS' office, Mary Elle realized how foolish she had acted. She felt like a teenager in trouble sitting in the principal's office. She was so embarrassed.

Thomas didn't say anything at first. He just sat there quietly, staring at them.

"What in the world happened?" He finally said. The look of disappointment on his face made Mary Elle shrink in her seat.

"It's this woman, Thomas. Get rid of her." Clarice said as she cried.

Mary Elle looked at her in disbelief. "Thomas, I am very sorry about what happened. I've never been in a situation like this before," Mary Elle said.

"I don't blame you. Not many people have been in a situation like this. Not many people have to deal with someone like Clarice," Thomas said.

"Are you seriously taking her side instead of your wife?"

"For the last time, you are not my wife, Clarice," Thomas said sternly but gently. Mary Elle could tell it pained him to say that, and she felt a bit of jealousy. Did he still have feelings for Clarice?

Clarice gasped in disbelief and stormed off. She was not used to not getting her way.

"Uncle Thomas," David, standing behind Thomas, quietly

finally spoke out. "We have to do something about it, Clarice. She can't waltz in here whenever she wants and wreak havoc. Clarice is not a part of this business. She sold her shares many years ago and lost any say in this business along with it."

Thomas sighed and rubbed his face with his hands. "You're right. If it weren't because of her condition, I would've told her to leave long ago."

"What condition?" David asked.

"She has cancer and is undergoing treatment. That is why she came back."

Mary Elle felt her stomach drop. She felt terrible for the way she had been with Clarice.

"I did not know, Thomas. I will apologize to her for my behavior the next time I see her." Mary Elle said.

"I appreciate that," Thomas said before turning to David and saying, "You're right. I will speak to her. She can't keep showing up like this."

Mary Elle excused herself and went to the bathroom to freshen up. She stared at herself in the mirror as she wiped the cake off her face.

She was in disbelief at the way she had acted. Mary Elle felt ashamed of the way she had dealt with the situation. She had never been in this sort of situation, but she should've never let Clarice get the best of her.

Now that she knew Clarice was battling cancer, she would be more understanding. She also decided to let Thomas go. It made sense that he would want to be there for Clarice. She needed him now. Mary Elle could wait until after Clarice finished her treatment. She would talk to Bailey tomorrow and tell her the camping trip would be a no-go.

* * *

A SPECIAL PACKAGE was waiting for Mary Elle when she got home. It was a beautiful wooden garden shelf with a very intricate hand-carved design for her front porch and a few starter kits from Melanie.

"Mom, when I saw this, I knew it would be perfect for you to enjoy your gardening. Love always, Mel." the note read.

She couldn't wait to have her kids visit this weekend for their camping trip. She needed some time to unwind and spend with her family. They always lifted her feelings when she was feeling down.

Rita wasn't able to make it after all. Robert was hospitalized after an atrial fibrillation episode. It had been terrifying. Mary Elle had driven over and spent time with Rita and Bob in the hospital before heading back to Willow Heights for the Grand Re-Opening. Bob was like a brother to Mary Elle. He had moved to their town in Helena Springs during their first year of high school. He and Rita have been inseparable since then.

CHAPTER 18

*A*fter a night of cleaning and baking, Mary Elle was ready to take on the rest of the week. She brought some of her special secret recipe muffins and coffees to share with the team.

She loved bringing them little surprises. Mary Elle knew Jasper loved coffee and that this would allow Lisa to enjoy her morning and not have to worry about baking and serving them. Thomas was there early and had the bright smile he was known for.

"Good morning, Thomas. Would you care for some coffee and a muffin?" Mary Elle asked.

"Don't mind if I do!" Thomas said smiling, "this is a pleasant surprise, Mary Elle. Thank you."

"I thought we all needed a little something after what we pulled off yesterday."

"I heard someone say there was coffee," Bailey said as she entered the staff kitchen.

It relieved Mary Elle to have Bailey join them. She didn't want to spend time alone with Thomas. She couldn't help her feelings for him, and she felt like a bit of distance was what she needed to do her job and let go of any illusions she ever had of having a relationship with him.

"You heard right. There are also muffins," Mary Elle said as she uncovered the muffins for Bailey to take her pick.

"These taste divine," Bailey said in between bites of the muffin.

"Hey Jasper, I brought you some coffee," Mary Elle said when she spotted Jasper putting his lunch in the refrigerator.

Jasper's face lit up. "Mary Elle, you've figured out the way to my heart. You know I can't say no to coffee!"

Mary Elle poured Jasper a cup and prepared coffee for the rest of the staff before heading to her office.

Today was going to be a busy day. New clients were trickling into the venue, their reputation grew, and the blog Britney wrote about Willow Acres was paying off. Brittney asked if she could come back again during the fall and winter months to blog about the other events the small town would host and include food and drink options.

Thomas was excited to see that not only was his business being reviewed, but other small businesses sprinkled all over Willow Heights. The other companies had also seen an increase in their revenue, which only meant great things for their town.

Mary Elle started working on her weekly project updates for Thomas and David when Bailey popped into her office.

"Mary Elle, I have great news!"

"Bailey, thank God you're here. I almost forgot to tell you; we need to put a pin on the camping trip with Thomas and the rest of the group."

"What? Why?" Bailey asked as she pushed her glasses up her nose.

"It's just not a good time right now."

"Honey, it's ok to feel nervous. You just came out of a marriage, but we all have such a great feeling about this."

ABIGAIL BECK

"What do you mean we?"

"That's what I came here to tell you. I already spoke to everyone about the camping trip. I only let the girls in on our secret about it being a way to get you and Thomas together. Everyone is so excited! The guys are excited too, but they love anything that has to do with the outdoors," Bailey said with a roll of her eyes.

"We have to come up with a way to cancel it," Mary Elle said as she rubbed her temple.

"Why? What's going on?" Bailey asked as she leaned forward.

"It's Clarice. The reason she's back is that she has cancer. Thomas has to be there for her. From my understanding, he's the only family she has."

"Mary Elle, my sister, works at the Cancer clinic in Winding Creek. If Clarice had cancer, we would all know about it. There are no other cancer centers nearby."

"What are you saying?"

"She's lying. Plain and simple," Bailey said as she crossed her arms and shook her head.

"Who would lie about something like that?"

"Clarice would," Bailey said with so much certainty that Mary Elle didn't dear question her.

* * *

MARY ELLE HADN'T BEEN able to process the information that Bailey had given her. She knew from Mrs. Adelman and many others that Clarice was no stranger to manipulating and lying, but this was too much.

She hoped for Thomas' sake that if she were genuinely lying, she would come clean. Although she wanted to say something, Mary Elle didn't think it was her place to say anything, especially because she didn't have any actual proof Clarice was lying.

"So, mom, how are you introducing Thomas to Michael?" Melanie teased her mother, "as your boyfriend or lover," she continued with a laugh.

Mary Elle hadn't mentioned the Clarice ordeal to any of her kids. She didn't want to make this weekend about that. She wanted to enjoy her time with them. It wasn't often that she got to have all three of them together.

Everett rolled his eyes and muttered something under his breath. Mary Elle could see that he regretted his decision to be a part of this trip.

"We're just friends, Mel. He is my boss."

"Not for much longer," Melanie said with a giggle. Everett let out a long groan, and Melanie shrunk in her seat. She was quiet for the rest of the ride.

Mary Elle couldn't put her finger on what was wrong with Everett. Had he fallen out of love with Melanie already? They barely spent time together, and their second anniversary had just passed.

* * *

ONCE THEY GOT to the campsite, they saw that Michael, DeeAnn, and Tiffany were there. They were pitching their tents, and DeeAnn was looking for wood to get the fire going.

They saw other families camping at a distance, and they found the lake and the trails that would lead to the mountaintop. Cellular reception was minimal. Everett complained about that immediately.

"Hey, honey! It's so good to see you!" Mary Elle said as she hugged her son, Michael.

"Hi mom, it's so good to see you," he said as he hugged her tightly.

"I've missed you so much," Mary Elle said, not wanting to let him go.

Her relationship with her daughters had only strengthened after the divorce, but things with Michael had been a little rocky. She knew he felt terrible about having known and not said anything before. He also said he wished he would've tried harder to convince Bill to come clean. Mary Elle knew better. Bill wasn't great at having hard conversations. The way things had worked out was his doing.

Thomas and the rest of the gang arrived soon after. Mary Elle was so nervous. She avoided Thomas and seeing him now interacting with her family only confused things. She caught up with DeeAnn and was happy to hear that her sister was completing everything to move to Willow Heights.

The air was fresh, yet it was so cozy with the smell of burning wood. It was magical.

"Here's some hot chocolate. Come sit by the fire with us," Tiffany said as she handed her mother and aunt mugs filled with hot chocolate and marshmallows.

DeeAnn and Mary Elle joined everyone by the fire. The sun had set, and it was getting chilly. Dean was strumming his guitar, and they huddled everyone around. She noticed Michael, Melanie and Ruby huddled in a corner talking, but she didn't see Everett anywhere.

Bailey came over with Patty, and while DeeAnn and Patty were deep into their conversation, Bailey pulled Mary Elle to the side.

"So, I asked my sister if Clarice had been in for treatment," Bailey said in a hushed tone.

"What did she say?"

"She said Clarice hasn't been back since her checkup a year ago."

"Are you sure? Maybe your sister just missed her?"

"Mary Elle, this is a tiny town. There's no way she would've missed her. My sister was the one that administered her radiation treatment when she got treated."

"Can you two stop gossiping over there and come join us?" Lisa called out playfully.

Mary Elle looked up and saw her waving her over with DeeAnn and Patty.

"Let's not say anything to anyone, okay?" Mary Elle said to Bailey before they made their way over. She spotted Michael and Thomas huddled together, and she wondered what they might be discussing.

They spent the rest of the night around the fire. They made S'Mores, told scary stories, and gathered around the fire singing. For dinner, Thomas made a delicious chili. It was perfect for a chilly night out under the stars.

THE FOLLOWING DAY, Mary Elle and Melanie got up earlier than the rest and made coffee and a light breakfast for everyone.

Before everyone else woke up, they went for a walk along the lake. It was breathtaking. Being in nature was so healing and refreshing.

"How are you feeling?" Mary Elle asked Melanie.

"I'm okay, mom. I'm enjoying spending time with you and everyone. I needed this break," she said, holding back tears. A lot was weighing her down that she was keeping to herself.

"We all needed this," Mary Elle said as they stood side by side watching the sunrise.

"The sound of the small waves is so relaxing," Melanie commented as she took a deep breath.

"It sure is. What would you like to do today?"

ABIGAIL BECK

"How about we learn to fish?" Melanie answered.

With a chuckle, Mary Elle said, "that sounds like fun,"

They stayed there for a few more minutes before Michael, Ruby, and Tiffany joined them. Tiffany was skipping rocks on the lake. Michael and Ruby chatted quietly while they fished.

Mary Elle heard Ruby giggling. She knew Michael was charming and funny. She wondered if he was finally seeing Ruby as a woman and not just as his little sister's friend.

Melanie noticed what Mary Elle was looking at and said, "You think something is going on there?"

"I don't know, but it wouldn't be a bad idea," Mary Elle said, smiling at Melanie.

"I think she likes him, but I can't tell with Michael," Melanie said.

"Young love," Mary Elle said as she watched them.

"There's something I have to tell you. I have yet to tell anyone," Melanie said. She couldn't hold this in any longer. She had to tell her mom.

"Sure, honey, why don't we go sit at that bench by the lake?" Mary Elle said.

Once seated on the bench, Melanie blurted out, "I'm late, and I think I might be pregnant," as she felt tears coming down her face.

"Why are you crying? That's great news, Melanie!" Mary Elle said as she pulled Melanie into another hug.

"I haven't taken the test yet, but I'm never late. I wanted to take a test while on the trip to surprise Everett. But he already left, and I'm apprehensive about how he will react."

"What worries you?"

"It has been tough to have many conversations with him lately. He's been very busy with work and has a lot of new projects."

"I understand. Marriage is hard work. When you get back

to New York, plan a special night for the two of you and talk to each other. Let him know how you are feeling."

Melanie couldn't tell her mother that she had tried that several times, but Everett canceled each time. She knew that her mother would worry about her and didn't want to burden her with her marriage problems.

Melanie didn't know how to deal with this anymore. Everett didn't even try to make things right when they fought almost every day. She was growing exhausted and tired of trying to make the marriage work. Melanie had also tried marriage counseling, but that didn't pan out with Everett's never-ending traveling and projects.

THEY SPENT the rest of the day fishing, canoeing, and playing card games with the gang. Thomas had left before Mary Elle had gotten back, and she was feeling kind of down about that.

She missed him. She had gotten used to having him around. Her kids let her know they liked Thomas. He was adventurous and had been fantastic with everyone there. He took the time to talk to everyone and get to know them. That was one of the things Mary Elle loved about him. There was no pretending with Thomas. He was genuinely a great person who wore his heart on his sleeve.

"Are you having a good time?" Michael asked as he slid in on the bench next to Mary Elle.

"I have my greatest three loves together again. How could I not be having a good time?"

"You seem happy, mom. Happier than I have ever seen you," Michael said as he studied her face.

"It's a different sort of happiness. I was always happy before, Mikey. You and your sisters filled me with so much joy, but after you all grew up, it felt as if my life lost meaning, and now, I'm finally living again, on my terms."

"It shows, and you do not know how relieved that makes me feel."

"None of this was your fault; you know that, right?"

"I know, but it doesn't make it any easier. Someone wants to talk to you, and I promised him I would take you to meet him."

"Who?"

"It's a surprise. Trust me; it's a good thing," Michael said, standing up.

"Okay, right now?"

"Yes," Michael said, holding his hand out for her.

CHAPTER 19

Mary Elle dried her hands on her sundress. She was nervous. Michael had blindfolded her and was leading her to meet who knows who. She hoped it wasn't Bill, but Michael seemed so excited about this that she didn't want to burst his bubble, so she just went along with him.

"We're here," she heard Michael say.

"Okay," she said as she felt Michael untie the blindfold. Once her blindfold came off, she saw the last person she expected to see standing before her. Michael kissed her cheek and headed back to the campsite.

"Hey there," Thomas said.

Mary Elle stood frozen in place. "Hi," was the only thing she got out.

"I've made us a little picnic," Thomas said as he guided her towards the lake. He was wearing jeans and a white button-down shirt with the sleeves rolled up to his elbows.

"I thought you had left," Mary Elle said as she followed him.

As the small picnic area came into view, Mary Elle let out a small gasp and said, "Thomas, this is so beautiful."

He had laid out a blanket with a few different cushions and a small breakfast tray with candles and flowers.

"I prepared it myself," he said with that boyish grin that made Mary Elle's heart skip a couple of beats. She studied the lines on his face. He was such a handsome man.

She could only imagine how good-looking he must have been at a young age. She was sure he must have been tough to resist. He was a handsome man, but he was also caring.

Mary Elle suddenly wished she had known him before. Before she met Bill and before he met Clarice. She shook her head to clear her mind. If she had never met Bill, she would not have her kids now.

"What's going on in that pretty head of yours?" Thomas asked.

"It's silly," Mary Elle said as she felt a blush coming on.

"Now I'm even more intrigued," Thomas said with a kind smile.

"Nothing but musings of what could have been," said Mary Elle.

Thomas nodded in understanding and smiled as he guided Mary Elle to the area he had set up for them.

As they sat down to enjoy their picnic. The effort Thomas had put into everything blew Mary Elle away. No one had ever made her feel so special. Thomas poured the wine and brought out an appetizer. The wine was delicious and sweet.

Everything seemed so perfect right now. Clarice popped into her head a few times, but she pushed it away. She would not let her ruin this moment.

"Thomas, I'm blown away by this picnic. You considered everything and made it exquisite."

"It's easy to get inspired and put out your best efforts when it's for someone like you, Mary Elle," he replied.

Mary Elle could feel herself blushing, and she felt butter-flies in her stomach. She had missed feeling this way.

For the first time in years, she felt loved, desired, and worthy of love and wanting. At this moment, Mary Elle knew she was falling in love with Thomas, and her feelings were undeniable.

Thomas cleared his throat and said, "Mary Elle, I have something to tell you."

"What is it?"

"I know things were strange because of Clarice, but I wanted you to be one of the first to know that I've ended all ties with her."

"What happened with Clarice?" Mary Elle asked, leaning forward. She wondered if she should tell him what she knew, but Thomas began speaking again before she had time to.

"Everything seemed off from the moment she came back. She mentioned nothing about being sick until later, and when I offered to take her to her treatments, she always refused. There were too many inconsistencies in her story, and then she started demanding financial help from me. Clarice has played me for a fool before, so I wanted to ensure she wasn't lying to me. I asked David to help me spy on her," Thomas said with a chuckle as he shook his head.

"Oh, my!" Mary Elle said, imagining him and David dressed in black like spies, and let out a small giggle.

"I asked Clarice the time and date of her next appoint-ment and confirmed her doctor's name and the facility. David and I rented a car and waited for her all day to show up, but she never did. David suggested we call the facility to double-check the appointment, so we did. The receptionist is Margie's grandniece, and she said Clarice hadn't been there in almost a year. My suspicions were right. She was lying to all of us."

"I am so sorry." Mary Elle said as she placed her hand

over his. Thomas was such a kind man; Clarice had known that and used it against him.

"That day, I also asked Jasper to monitor her house and check if her car was there. It turns out she left in the morning around 11:30 AM and went to brunch. After that, she went shopping and then home," Thomas said.

"You were at the facility all day?" Mary Elle asked

"Yes, David and I were there if she showed up, but she never did. When Jasper called us to tell us she was back home, we went there. As I was pulling into her driveway, she was coming outside and wasn't expecting to see us there. We asked her if we could go inside, and she said yes. Once we were inside, I asked her how her doctor's appointment had gone. She sat down and just stared at me. Clarice knew I had caught her in her web of lies." Thomas stood then and paced. "She finally said she didn't go to the doctor because they had rescheduled her appointment. Then I asked her where she had gone all day, and she said she had been at home. As I sat there and looked around, I could see the shopping bags were still in the den, and I pointed it out to her. She had been to all her favorite stores and had not been home all day, as she was claiming. I told her I knew the truth. I knew she didn't have cancer. There was never a doctor's appointment or treatment she was going to. I told her I didn't want her coming around anymore. I had uncovered all her lies and deceptions, and I did not want to be a part of it anymore," Thomas said with a firm conviction of his actions and decision.

Mary Elle was at a loss for words. What could she say or do to make Thomas feel better? She stood and made her way to him.

"Wow. Thomas... I'm speechless. I knew something seemed off, but I never thought she would lie about that. Why would she lie?"

"Clarice said she lied because she knew she was losing

me. She said someone told her about you and that she knew that if she didn't act fast, she would lose me forever."

"What do you mean?"

"I might have told someone I had feelings for you, and that person told her," Thomas said.

"You have feelings for me?" Mary Elle asked in disbelief. Thomas liked her. He told someone he had feelings for her. She began to smile, and she felt guilty because it obviously upset Thomas that Clarice had been lying.

Thomas got closer to her, looked into her eyes, and said, "My world hasn't been the same since the day I saw you having lunch with your daughters," He took her hands in his and continued, "I knew it then like I know it now that I want you in my life. The moment you stepped into my life, you added color to it. My world was gray before I met you. I knew I had to deal with Clarice to move forward with you. I want a future with you, Mary Elle."

Mary Elle was having a hard time forming a sentence. She stood there, sure that she was smiling like a fool, but she didn't care. Thomas had feelings for her, too. She hadn't imagined it.

Clarice was now a bad dream left somewhere in the past, and their future together would be full of love with no guilt or intruders trying to steal their joy.

"That is if this is what you want too?" Thomas said, grinning, his smile matching hers.

"I'll have to think about it." She said with a sly smile.

Now it was Thomas' turn to be at a loss for words. Mary Elle burst out in a fit of giggles when she saw the confused look on his face.

"Thomas, I would love nothing more than a future with you," Mary Elle said, squeezing his hands.

He smiled then and leaned in and kissed her. She wrapped her arms around his neck and kissed him, too.

Mary Elle felt as if she was spinning. She was on cloud nine. She couldn't wipe the smile off her face, but that was okay because Thomas couldn't stop smiling either. When their lips parted, they stood there staring into each other's eyes, their foreheads pressed against each other.

Mary Elle's stomach grumbled, and she quickly jumped away from Thomas in embarrassment.

Thomas laughed, "May you please join me for a delicious feast prepared by yours truly?" he asked as he motioned over to the blanket.

"I'd love nothing more," Mary Elle said as she took his hand, making their way back to the blanket together.

EPILOGUE

Summer had been great in Willow Heights, but Fall had always been Mary Elle's favorite season. She loved the way the trees changed colors, wearing cozy sweaters and boots.

Today she and Thomas would head out to a town nearby. The town was smaller than Willow Heights, but they hosted an annual rodeo. She had never been to a rodeo and had never square danced before either.

Mary Elle felt rejuvenated when she was with Thomas. She always had the goofiest smile when she thought of him. They had been seeing each other for a few weeks now, and things were going very well.

Clarice hadn't come back since everyone found out she had been lying. She was nothing more than a distant memory now. Mary Elle had come clean to Thomas knowing that Clarice had been lying before he told her. She didn't want to hide anything from him or have anything ruin their relationship. It didn't upset Thomas that she knew and hadn't told him. He said he was glad he could figure it out on his own.

She couldn't believe it when she thought back on how

much her life had changed in the last year. She was the happiest she'd ever been. Mary Elle finally knew what it was like to be appreciated in a relationship. Thomas made her feel special by always considering her thoughts and opinions.

She was working and depending on herself. All the things she had now she had earned by herself. No one was ever going to come and turn her world upside down again. She would never, ever give anyone that type of power over life.

Her kids were also doing great. Tiffany had graduated with honors and had landed a great job at an up-and-coming hotel in North Carolina. Michael was making a name for himself and would soon make partner at his firm. Melanie had won several awards for her editorial projects. She had finally convinced Everett to take a trip together, where she would surprise him with the news that she was pregnant.

Rita and Bob visited Willow Heights, and Bob fell in love with the little town. They were now looking into buying their retirement home here. Thomas had taken Bob on a fishing trip on his boat; the two had hit it off as if they'd known each other their whole lives. Mary Elle hadn't spoken to Bill, but she knew from the kids that he and Barbara were still going strong.

Mary Elle glanced at her clock and realized she had to hurry if she would be ready by the time Thomas said he'd be picking her up.

She didn't know what to wear, but she thought a good pair of jeans and some boots with a pretty top would make the perfect outfit. She did her makeup and hair and kept things pretty natural. Even her makeup had changed since she came to live in Willow Heights.

Every day, she felt more comfortable in her skin. She no longer had to keep up her appearance, and she knew no one would judge her if she didn't have a full face of makeup on. Life in Willow Heights had taught her to let go and to relax.

A light knock on her front door caught her off guard. She looked at the clock on the wall and figured Thomas must be early.

When Mary Elle opened the door, it wasn't Thomas standing there.

"Mel, what are you doing here? Is everything okay?"

Melanie couldn't get a word out; she just burst into tears. Mary Elle pulled her into her arms.

"Honey, did something happen to Everett?" Mary Elle asked as she pulled Melanie inside the house.

"No, mom... he left me."

"What?"

"I told him I was pregnant, and he left me," Melanie said as the tears streamed down her face, "He said he didn't want to have kids and would sign his rights away."

Mary Elle was speechless. This was a new low for Everett. How could he abandon his child?

"It's ok, honey. You're here now. Everything will be okay," Mary Elle said as she hugged Melanie tighter. Mary Elle didn't know what the future held, but if she'd learned anything at all this past year, it was that we could make all the plans we wanted, but God always knows exactly what we need, and he would always provide.

THANK you for reading New Beginnings in Willow Heights. I hope you enjoyed it! The next book in the series, Finally Home in Willow Heights, can be found here. Click here for the third book in the series, Christmas in Willow Heights.

Let's be friends!

Join Abigail's Newsletter for reminders of upcoming releases.

Join Abigail's Reader Group for: First Looks, exclusive giveaways, and more!

Printed in Great Britain
by Amazon